FLAME

Desire... Vengeance

P. C. BALASUBRAMANIAN

INDIA • SINGAPORE • MALAYSIA

ISBN 979-8-89067-866-9

Disclaimer

This is a work of fiction. All names, characters, businesses, places, events and incidents in this book are the product of the author's imagination or used in a fictitious manner. Any resemblance to persons, living or dead is purely coincidental.

Dedicated to every reader in any part of the world who is still in the habit of picking up a book despite many other distractions and avenues to spend time.

“There is something exciting about Bala’s writing. His visualisation of the characters is very interesting and his concept is indeed fresh. I particularly liked the backdrop of the dental world. The way he weaves two different characters from two different worlds and sets the stage for a thrilling and unexpected climax truly sets the pace of the narrative.

As a film maker, I could visualise every scene as a film, who knows, I may even love to adapt it to the screen.”

– Suresh Krissna, Film Director

“Intriguing plot and narrative, a short fiction that has all elements to keep the readers engaged. I read it in one go. Loved it.”

– Ravi Subramanian, Author

CONTENTS

PARTHIBAN

The city was asleep. It was still and silent, barring the sounds of a few urchins moving around and stray dogs barking at something new or alien to them. Even food delivery agents had retired after delivering their last order. The sky was a deep grey with scattered dark clouds shrouding the moon from bearing witness to whatever was happening below.

Parthiban was wide awake in his small one-room abode provided by the Slum Clearance Board. He was watching the movie BABA on Sun TV. His most favourite actor, his idol, Superstar Rajinikanth, was delivering his signature dialogue with a knife in his hand: "Khatham, khatham, mudinjathu mudinju pochu (Khatham, khatham, what is over is over)". Normally, Parthiban would have clapped for this scene even if he was watching it alone at home, but he was not his usual self. He whispered to himself. "Sorry, Thalaiva, what is over is not over... I have to complete a task... I have to avenge... I have to ruin him! I have an agenda to kill him tomorrow. Forgive me..." He knew that this would be the last time he would be watching a TV programme. Tomorrow everyone would watch him on TV—soon, he would be the newsmaker; he would be the one trending on social media; he would be committing the first, and hopefully, the last, murder of his life.

He dialled a number from his mobile and said softly, "Sleep well tonight, my dear, from tomorrow you will have a very bright future." At the other end, there was absolute silence, and then, a few stifled sobs. She knew she would be picked up late the next evening for a task—one that Parthiban had been mentally bracing himself for over the last few days.

Parthiban opened the drawer of the dusty, old table and picked up something that was encased in faded white cloth. Unwrapping it, he looked at the gleaming knife and ran his finger along its sharp edge and pointed tip. He thrust the knife into the air in a stabbing motion, practising for the following night.

He gulped three pegs of the cheap brandy he had procured a few hours back, smoked two cigarettes back-to-back, and ate his favourite chicken biriyani.

Though he had nothing to lose—he had been told by his doctor that he would not live beyond a year because of lung cancer—he now had something to win...

Smiling to himself, he spread the mat on the floor and attempted to sleep. His eyes remained closed but he was far from sleep.

* * * * *

KALPANA

Two years ago...

Kalpana was nervous as well as excited. She was opening her second dental clinic 'Kalpana Dental Care' at Alwarpet, a prime locality in Chennai. Her first clinic was running just fine at Tambaram, a Southern suburb of Chennai. She had opened her first clinic after working at a reputed dental clinic for a year, after completing her MDS. Although she was earning some revenue, she was not making enough money to make her venture profitable. She wasn't able to draw funds to the extent she wanted. Based on the advice of well-wishers, she borrowed from the bank, pledging their only property—the house she was living in with her dad and her little daughter, who was just three years old.

Kalpana was single. She had not married. She had been ditched by her senior in the college with whom she had had an affair. Her ex-boyfriend and the father of her daughter, Dr Agathiyan, was politically powerful and affluent. He was a key member of the powerful political party, Namathu Puratchi Katchi (Our Revolutionary Party), which was the chief Opposition Party then. They had not been on the ruling side for the last two terms. There was a time when they were the most powerful party in the State but now held the Opposition status. The change in the thinking of the voting population didn't favour their agenda, strategy and leadership.

Kalpana had lost a lot in life. Being deprived of a good personal life haunted her constantly. She nursed a grudge against Agathiyan for ditching her and choosing to marry a woman from another political family. That union had been orchestrated primarily for political reasons by Agathiyan's father, Elangovan, for whom power and position were prime factors that influenced every decision.

Agathiyan was also not apologetic. When he explained to Kalpana his inability to go against his father's veto, he had even shamelessly offered to retain Kalpana as his mistress—apparently, that had been his father's recommendation too. Kalpana would never forget the miserable feeling she had experienced then. She had walked away from him without uttering a single word. Pride and humiliation had prevented her from continuing the conversation with Agathiyan. Pregnant with his child, she had not allowed Agathiyan to see her feelings of despair and abandonment.

Her thirst to be a successful professional and become rich and famous grew more intense after she was ditched. Her father, who was aware of her relationship with Agathiyan, had warned her that it was dangerous and unsafe for middle-class folk to hope for a liaison with a political family He was aware of the pedigree of the political party. He knew the immoral, unethical and absolute disregard for values that the party and its founding members had. He was certain that Agathiyan would be no exception.

Kalpana regretted that she had ignored her father's advice. The end result was her tarnished personal life. Her father's health had been deteriorating ever since. She was, after all, his only child—a brilliant student and a very beautiful woman. A clever, intelligent achiever who foolishly fell for Agathiyan's charm; an affair that ended in complete disaster.

The new clinic was inaugurated by Dr Sanjeev Jain, her super senior in dental college and currently, a renowned dentist in the city. Dr Jain was aware of Kalpana's personal situation and had a soft corner for her, even though she was a potential competitor. He spent a few minutes offering her tips on running the clinic effectively. He advised her on how to increase her clientele and secure an income from other sources, especially from healthcare companies whose products were associated with dental care.

After the simple launch, Kalpana instructed her assistant, Meena, to arrange packed food for the few invitees. Sixteen-year-old Meena had been with Kalpana the past couple of years, assisting her at the clinic as well as at home. Kalpana took care of Meena's education through distance learning and paid for her upkeep. Two years ago, a depressed, helpless and motherless Meena had been referred to Kalpana for financial support. Since then, Kalpana had been taking care of her.

Meena had come to Kalpana in a state of mental trauma but was much better now after two years in Kalpana's care.

* * * * *

KALPANA

Four years ago...

A young Kalpana had taken up MDS at the popular, Madras Dental College, in Chennai. She didn't get admission to study medicine in a government-run medical college, and considering the steep price she would have to pay to get into a private medical college, she opted to study dentistry. Having completed her Bachelor's degree from a college in Coimbatore (the city in which her father had retired from service), she embarked on MDS, as she was keen to complete her post-graduation. She opted to live in the hostel as her home was far away from the college, though she made it a point to go home and spend time with her dad over the weekends.

Her class had one hundred and twenty students, with equal numbers of boys and girls. Fortunately for her, three friends from her previous college—Shalini, Sharmila and Uma—also joined the course with her, so she had the company of friends from day one. The special bond that exists among girls of that age is difficult to explain in words. It is best experienced in person. Kalpana liked the atmosphere of the college, though the hostel facilities were not up to the mark. On requesting the hostel authorities, Uma and Sharmila became her roommates.

In the entire class, Kalpana stood out, primarily because of her striking good looks. She was tall with large-brown eyes, dark, naturally-arched eyebrows, luminous complexion, long hair, thick pink lips and enviable curves. She would have won the Miss Madras Dental College contest hands down, had there been any such event. Every guy wanted to befriend her. Some did not dare to even introduce themselves. Some girls were envious of her beauty and stayed away from her. Kalpana liked the attention. She knew the power of her looks. However, she had ignored advances from all the gawking guys, till she met Agathiyan at a college event.

Kalpana was not just good at academics. She was gifted with a good singing voice that made her popular among friends. She used to sing on demand in the hostel. Many of her friends encouraged her to represent first-year MDS students at the college's annual meet. She used to sing often as a young schoolgirl and had enjoyed the applause from a friendly audience of schoolmates and teachers. But to sing before this audience? They'd start judging her the moment she stepped on stage before she struck the first note!

It was an intra-college festival and students from every batch, under-graduation to post-graduation, could use this platform to present their skills. The variety of performances was diverse—competitions ranged from poetry recitation to mono-acting, skits, singing, stand-up comedy, and dancing. The event was very popular—

the packed auditorium roared not only with thunderous applause but also equal measures of booing. When juniors performed especially, the seniors waited for a chance to boo them.

It was Kalpana's turn. Trying to conceal her anxiety, she walked on stage. She had chosen to wear a black chiffon saree with a black short-sleeved blouse. Her well-shampooed hair flowed like beautiful waves, the curls at the end bouncing with every step. The black saree accentuated her glowing complexion. Her experience in draping the saree was evident from the neat pleats and the graceful, perfect fall. She carried herself with poise and elegance as she walked up to the mike. Some of the seniors who had booed when they heard that she was a first-year MDS student, were stunned into silence when they saw her on stage. For many, including several guys who were still doing their BDS, she instantly became their 'dream girl'. Their fantasies varied—some wanted to marry her at once, some visualized her as a life partner at a later point in life, some wanted to take her to bed immediately, and some just wanted to be friends. There was not a single person in that room, male or female, who could overlook her.

Agathiyan, who was lounging in the last row with his group of friends, stood up and walked closer to the stage, much to the surprise of his gang. He always had an entourage with him—a group of students who were more accomplices and sycophants than friends. Though he was in the third year, the members of his entourage included students from every batch except the first year. His 'friends' knew that since Agathiyan 'eyed' Kalpana, they would have to keep a safe distance from her from then on.

Agathiyan could easily pass off as a silver-screen hero. He was tall and well-muscled—a body lovingly honed through regular running and enthusiastic visits to the gym. Despite his brown skin, his face always had a radiance. A heavy stubble only added to his rugged good looks. Thanks to his affluent background, he could afford expensive brands—in clothing, accessories, bikes and cars. Many girls were attracted to him, but fearing his background and connections, they stayed away.

Notwithstanding this, there were two girls, one from the third year and another from the fourth year, whom he dated secretly and had physical relationships with, whenever he had the chance. He had the looks of a well-mannered hero and kept his other not-so-heroic side well hidden. Though he was in the third year of MDS, he rarely attended college till he met Kalpana at the event.

Many students who knew him were surprised to see Agathiyan standing and watching Kalpana. Kalpana rendered a beautiful number, one of maestro Ilayaraja's hits. When she finished singing, she received a standing ovation and thunderous applause from the audience. Agathiyan walked up to the stage appropriating a huge bouquet from a table reserved for special guests.

With a confident swagger and the arrogance of power and wealth, he walked up to Kalpana and presented her with the bouquet. "I am Agathiyan. I am smitten with you—what a singer you are! And you look ravishing," he whispered into Kalpana's ears.

Kalpana was thrilled with the rousing response she received. She also silently relished the special whisper from the handsome Agathiyan. She was unaware of his background till then. She had no inkling that her life was about to change. And how!

* * * * *

KALPANA

Now...

Kalpana was getting ready to leave for her clinic. She had been busy making a few phone calls. The interest on her bank loan was due for the last quarter, and the bank was applying pressure on her, but she concealed her stress and portrayed an image of a confident, suave and stylish medical professional. In her spare time, she distracted herself with social media, especially Facebook and Instagram. She had many followers on Instagram, people who waited for her to post pictures and brief videos. Though her videos mostly related to dental care, she also made sure she posted other videos featuring her songs, fashion tips and even a few dance reels. She enjoyed the adulation of over eight thousand followers, seventy per cent of whom were male.

Her father sensed her distress. “Kalpana, I am worried about your investment. These days we have a dentist on every street. How are you going to make your clinics successful?” He was concerned for their future. “You could have taken up a job in some hospital. I know you do not like it, but see, we are middle-class people.” He continued, “How are you going to safeguard this house? I am worried. This is the only asset we have, and the only one that will take care of your child in the future..."

"Appa, please stop!" Kalpana cut in sharply. "Your property will be safe. I know how to take care of my child. You please stay out of my business. If you feel you don't want to risk your property, let me know... I will find some alternative."

She immediately regretted her words and tone. She knew that her father's concern was justified and that he was extra anxious on account of her messed-up personal life. She tried to make amends by walking up to her father and taking his hands in hers. "Appa," she said gently. "Trust me... Someday I will make it very big. This is my only agenda in life. You will live to see it. Please bless me." She took her father's hand and placed it on her head. Her father remained silent.

She went back to the dressing table to ensure she was looking good. She had paired her cream-and-black checked shirt with black trousers. She picked up a comb and ran it through her curls. Her makeup was so minimal, it looked like she had not used any. Satisfied with what she saw, she stepped out. She got into her second-hand Maruti Swift and, with her earphones on, she called the bank to convey that she would pay the interest within fifteen days. She was buying time.

When she reached her new clinic in Alwarpet, she was dismayed. There were no appointments fixed, meaning no income for the day. She managed to hide her anxiety behind a veil of calm nonchalance. Yet, she knew she needed a solution quickly.

* * * * *

ELANGOVAN

Namathu Puratchi Katchi (Our Revolutionary Party) party headquarters.

Unusually, there was heavy traffic on the road to the headquarters of Namathu Puratchi Katchi political party. Elangovan, the party chief, was expected to attend a meeting after a long time. Ever since he had developed health issues related to the heart, he rarely visited. But this day was important. The assembly elections were upcoming in the next twelve months and no stone could be left unturned to ensure a victory. Many subjects had to be discussed, some with several party members, some with close party members, and some secretly with other parties for possible alliances. There were also other matters—monetary considerations, the selection of candidates based on caste and community, and the ability of the candidates to spend money on their respective constituencies.

Elangovan was dressed in his political attire. Starched white full-sleeved shirt, spotless white dhoti with the party flag colours on the border, and a matching 'angavastram' worn over one shoulder. If he had a choice, he would have preferred wearing regular clothes like jeans or trousers with shirts. But he knew politicians in Tamil Nadu were expected to dress in a particular way.

The entire area was flooded with people in white, dressed just like him. Many vehicles were inconsiderately and wrongfully parked outside the compound on the busy road, causing inconvenience to the general public. The public, trying to navigate past the place in their cars and bikes cursed party members in the most unparliamentary language. But silently. They didn't dare question aloud the arrogance and surly attitudes of the party members for fear of being abused or beaten.

Elangovan had an agenda. He wanted to nominate his son, Agathiyan, as the chief ministerial candidate though Agathiyan had never held the position of even an MLA before. He had lost the election last time, like many in the party. But, in this matter, Elangovan was on a sticky wicket. According to the grapevine, many within the party were not in favour of Agathiyan. They preferred the ailing Elangovan to run for CM. But Elangovan was well aware that there was a poor chance of him lasting the term on account of his debility. He had a clear agenda that his son should be promoted to the position while he was still alive.

The party was rich. It was believed to be the fifth richest party in the country, with many assets and cash safely held under a Trust of which Elangovan and his family members were the major trustees. This didn't include several other assets including real estate, finance, transport and media companies in the country. In addition, cash was parked with a few private equity firms outside the country. Of course, the sources for such investments could never be disclosed for obvious reasons.

As Elangovan's white Lexus approached the office headquarters, there were loud slogans of "Vazhga Thalaivar! Vazhga Tamil Nadu!" A proud Elangovan, seated on the modified front seat, waved royally despite the pain and discomfort he felt all over his body. The greed for power overcame his physical debility. He was delighted to see several posters all over the median on the road. His son's picture was a part of some of these posters, but in some of them, his son's picture was missing—conspicuously and surprisingly.

Elangovan was aware of the political game being played by the senior members of his own party. He suspected Karadi Kathiresan—the perceived second-in-command, preferred both by the people and some of the party members—was also involved in this game. 'Karadi' meaning "bear', was the prefix given by Kathiresan's supporters. This prefix was given to him based on his own story that at the age of fourteen, he had confronted and driven away a bear single-handedly in his village. The veracity of this story was suspect—there was no evidence to corroborate it—but the prefix served very well, to convey his strength, power and agility.

Elangovan knew he would have to deal with Karadi appropriately without damaging the relationship and without disrupting his dream of promoting his son. He also knew that it would be difficult to push the case in favour of his son. Agathiyan did not have a good reputation. His name had been tarnished after the death of his wife, Amutha, under suspicious circumstances a year ago.

Amutha was believed to have committed suicide after years of undisclosed and untreated depression. But there were rumours afloat, not without reason, that she was killed by Agathiyan because she became aware of some of his secrets. Some believed that Agathiyan had silenced her when she threatened to interfere with his Casanova lifestyle. A few yellow journalists had written lurid stories around her death, but no cases had been registered against Agathiyan.

Even Elangovan suspected that Agathiyan had a hand in it, yet he was determined to protect his son and his tribe. This meant that women's votes would be lost if Agathiyan was fielded as the candidate for CM. Karadi Kathiresan had already prepared a few of his loyalists within the party to play this trump card so that he would be next in line for the king's throne. After all, he had been waiting many years for it. His only hindrance was Agathiyan. Luckily for him, Elangovan had stopped with only one legitimate child.

* * * * *

KALPANA

The pressure was getting to Kalpana. Her inability to service the bank loan and pay the interest could jeopardize her position. Her father's only property, which would eventually become hers, was at risk though the quantum of loan was not high. She could easily increase her loan against this property and open another clinic, if not more. Yet, if the investment did not yield returns the situation could become worse.

Her current earnings were just enough to maintain the three of them—her daughter, her father and herself. Her father had minimal requirements. However, when it came to Kalpana it was a different story. She was used to certain standards. She was already compromising on luxuries like designer clothing and accessories, cosmetics, and visits to top-notch spas and beauty salons. These were indulgences she used to take for granted. She was also unable to buy a new car. She felt she was merely surviving and not really living. This attitude led to her avoiding several social events, including dinner and party invitations from fellow professionals.

She rose wearily from her seat and walked into the wash area. Squeezing a small bit of facewash into her palm, she scrubbed till her face felt squeaky clean. She buried her face in a fresh towel and felt her exhaustion slip away. She scrutinized herself critically in the mirror. She couldn't help a slight smile of satisfaction at the image she saw. Her skin was flawless; not a single hair had greyed. Her slender nose and full lips only enhanced her beauty. She then picked up her favourite perfume and applied it on her wrist, below the ears, and on her throat and nape. She felt rejuvenated. The mirror image motivated her, increased her confidence, and fuelled her desire to do well in life.

Agathiyan was certainly lucky to have had her as an exclusive possession for all those years. They had had a blissful, wild time as long as they were together. One had to grant this to Agathiyan—he knew how to make a lady feel special. The long drives, the fancy restaurants, the expensive gifts, and his prowess in bed—all contributed to Kalpana being on cloud nine while the relationship lasted. Two years her senior, they had continued their relationship even after he finished college. It was only when she became pregnant and sought a commitment from him that he dumped her. She sighed. Now she felt a vacuum.

As she came out of the wash area and reached her consulting seat, she was surprised to see a handsome man waiting for her. He stood up when he saw her and natural instinct made both of them survey each other quickly, without a word. He was in a black Chinese-collared shirt and had folded up the sleeves casually. He was fair-complexioned with a chiselled chin. A three-day-old stubble added to his charm. He had gelled his long hair and combed it back neatly. His slim waist highlighted his broad shoulders. The thick black frame that held the lens of his glasses further boosted his looks, giving him an air of dignity, intelligence and respectability. There was no denying that his presence had an instant impact on Kalpana. She found him desirable.

"Hello, Doc. I am Suraj Chander. Sorry, I had to come to you without a prior appointment. I hope that is fine?" As he spoke, he shook his hands with Kalpana, looking directly into her eyes. His grip was firm and strong; she loved the feeling.

"That's perfectly fine. I am Dr Kalpana."

"Of course, I know your name. I saw the board outside and that's why I am here."

"Oh yes, of course. Please sit down. Tell me, what can I do for you?" Kalpana went directly to the subject, though she found his eyes very distracting and his presence coming in the way of her concentration.

"It's this toothache of mine, Doc. For the last three days it's been terrible. My regular dentist is on vacation and I can't bear to wait, considering the discomfort and pain. I was on my way to work when I saw your clinic and walked in. Thankfully, you are here."

Kalpana was happy that she had just had a good face wash before she saw him. She caught herself wondering if his dentist friend was a woman or a man but, obviously, she couldn't ask him that. She thought she must be going crazy, but she was somehow feeling light and good.

"Please sit here," she said making Suraj lean back in the dentist's chair. As she adjusted the seat, she interrogated him on his age, his eating habits, whether he smoked, how often he drank, whether he was diabetic, etc. Her profession gave her the liberty to ask such questions, providing an opportunity to know more about him in the process.

"Oh, I am not diabetic, Doc! I exercise every day. I sweat it out at the gym regularly." He patted his arm to indicate he had good biceps. "I am vegan. Yes, I do drink once or twice a week—only single malt. But why do you ask me if I smoke or drink, Doc? Just curious..."

"In case you need a root canal or a tooth extraction, I need these details to evaluate how local anaesthesia will work," Kalpana replied glibly, without revealing just how nosy she was about his personal life. The more she observed him, the more she was impressed with his looks, toned body and easy confidence.

As she leaned closer to examine his teeth, she could smell his cologne. Though she didn't recognize it, she found it heady and intoxicating. With an effort, she reminded herself that this was professional proximity and that she should focus on the job at hand. While she carried out her professional scrutiny, Suraj couldn't resist getting a close look at her. He liked her short shirt and the skinny jeans she was wearing. He noticed that she had a slender waist and slim legs, and was reasonably tall. Her perfectly filled-out cheeks with high cheekbones were glowing, and her large, brown eyes were too attractive to go unnoticed.

Kalpana noticed Suraj checking her out. She didn't really mind it—in fact, she rather enjoyed it. She too felt slightly turned on when she touched his cheeks, parts of his face and lips, in the process of examining his teeth.

"Oh man, you do need to get a root canal done," she said, touching his wisdom tooth with her dental scraper.

"Ahhh!" Suraj yelped when she pried his decaying tooth.

"See? This pain will not only increase but will get worse as the tooth festers. And the infection will spread to the neighbouring teeth if you don't attend to it."

"When can we do it?" Suraj asked. "I have a lot of travel coming up. I can't afford to postpone..."

"I'll prescribe some medicines for now. We can do the root canal in three days. Let me also take some measurements post the procedure, to get you a nice ceramic crown."

"Wow, I am going to be crowned!" Suraj laughed and continued, "As what? Mr Chennai?" He winked at Kalpana.

"Why not?" Kalpana responded with a twinkle in her eye.

She then explained the process in detail, the professional fee and the cost of the crown. Suraj understood and agreed to it all.

"You can travel after a week or so—that's my assurance to you. You can even smile at people more confidently." Kalpana cheered him up.

Suraj left the clinic after handing over his business card that read:

Suraj Chander
Partner
Green Stream Venture India
Chennai. Bangalore. Mumbai. Dubai. Mauritius

Kalpana was impressed, and the business card found its way to her pouch, but only after she stored his mobile number.

* * * * *

AGATHIYAN

Agathiyan was driving along the highway. He ignored the few calls he received on his mobile—calls from party colleagues. His phone was connected to the car's audio system through Bluetooth. These calls were not important to him.

He was in a very excited mood and his adrenaline was flowing. For some time now, he had been targeting Vanita, a TV actor and anchor. He had first met her at an awards ceremony where he had been invited as the chief guest. Vanita had received the Best Actress award for the year at that event, and Agathiyan had instantly fallen for her height, long hair, not-thin-not-plump-just-right figure, and for her dusky complexion. Playboy that he was, he kept falling for the fair sex and constantly sought variety.

He dialled Parthiban, the man whose additional job it was to make arrangements in the farmhouse situated around forty kilometres away from Chennai city. The farmhouse was intentionally designed to look ordinary from the outside with an almost bare garden with only a few coconut and mango trees and a pathway that extended to a villa inside.

Once you entered the villa, it could easily be rated as one of the finest. With its polished marble flooring, luxurious fittings, expensive furniture and large paintings, the house smacked of money, if not taste. Contributing to the opulence was a huge home theatre, a large bar and a dance floor. Of the four bedrooms, one was reserved exclusively for Agathiyan. The bar was stocked with the best of whiskey, vodka, wine and beer from all over the world. A designer humidor stacked with Cuban cigars was prominently visible.

Parthiban picked up the call. "Aiyya (sir), please tell me..."

"Hope she has reached?" Agathiyan was keen to ensure that there was no room for any mess-up.

"Yes, Aiyya. I brought her here around half an hour back."

"Is she happy?"

"I don't know, Aiyya. She was silent while she was in the car—only asked if you come here often."

Agathiyan smiled and asked Parthiban what he had said in reply.

"I said you come here only with friends for parties Aiyya, and also for yoga." Parthiban grinned at the other end.

"Ha ha! You are super, Parthiban... Fine, wait there. Once I reach you can leave after cooking something for us. Don't forget the Ginger Chicken for my drinks." Agathiyan pushed the accelerator further. The car was speeding at 130 km per hour.

After he zipped into the farmhouse, he went inside to see Vanita. He was delighted to see her in a black gown that generously revealed her well-rounded and pushed-up breasts. She had tied her hair loosely, knowing that it would get undone sooner or later. The entire room smelled fresh, thanks to the gel she used for showering and the perfume she had sprayed lavishly all over herself.

Agathiyan welcomed her warmly with a smile, and despite his desire to immediately take her to the bed, he opted for a shower. He wanted her to feel good and excited as well.

"Babe, just give me ten minutes, I'll join you soon. Let's have some drinks and a great time together. You are just ravishing and I am going to ..." He didn't complete the sentence, but ran his lips lustily over hers. He went into his bedroom, threw away the dhoti that bore the party flag colour as a border, removed his shirt and innerwear and sank into the tub that had been already prepared for him.

Parthiban was busy cooking a special meal. He knew he would earn a good tip that evening as his boss was very happy. Last time, a month ago, his boss had not been pleased as the lady he had brought was uncooperative, disinterested, and reluctant to indulge him. Parthiban knew that what he was doing was nothing but pimping, and he was not proud of it. But he needed the job, and the money.

He needed to provide for his daughter. So, he silenced his conscience and concentrated on pleasing his boss.

Parthiban completed his work in the kitchen, arranged all the food nicely on the dining table, filled ice cubes for the single malt and waited for his boss to give him further instructions.

Agathiyan emerged from his bedroom, looking dashing in a dark blue Polo and khaki shorts. His damp, carelessly slicked-back hair enhanced his looks. He walked Parthiban to the main door to send him off and tipped him heavily.

"Parthiban, I will give you more the day I get Maya. That bitch is acting pricey just because she had a couple of box-office hits. Also, remember you will get more if I get the very young ones..." He had a leer on his face as he spoke.

Parthiban took the money and left, knowing that he would have to return the next day at 8:00 AM to take Vanita back. He cursed his boss in his thoughts but had to be part of these dirty episodes—there was no escape. He was especially disgusted with Agathiyan's lust for innocent young girls. Parthiban was worried about who would be his next victim.

Agathiyan fixed a double large Hibiki whiskey and offered a glass of Spanish Garnacha red wine to Vanita. Before she took the glass, he put both glasses down, gave her a tight hug and kissed her passionately. She kissed him back. He buried his face in her neck and as he moved his face lower towards the exposed bulge, she pushed him gently and said, "Let's enjoy the drink, dear. We have enough time, and you are in a great mood."

"Of course, I have been waiting eagerly for you," Agathiyan replied instantly.

"What is so special in me?" Vanita fished for compliments.

"Whatever you have covered with this beautiful gown."

Both laughed, and as they settled down with their drinks, Vanita said, "Agathiyan sir, I hope I can become a heroine soon on celluloid. I hope you will help me through your contacts with production houses. Parthiban told me that you have a lot of influence there."

"Definitely dear, anything for you. And do call me Agathiyan when we are alone...avoid calling me 'sir' as that creates a distance."

A night of passion and lustful lovemaking followed until 2:00 AM.

* * * * *

ELANGOVAN

"Where have you been? I've been trying to reach you since last evening. I rang several times!" Elangovan asked Agathiyan with a mix of concern and irritation. Agathiyan had just reached home in the morning.

"I went for a private party, Appa, and by mistake, I left the phone at home here in silent mode. Sorry about it." Agathiyan continued, "But what's the issue?"

"We have barely eight months to go before the election, and it is about time we planned our strategy. You need to cut down your activities," Elangovan cautioned Agathiyan without dwelling on the details. "Remember, the media will be after you. Somehow, you managed to evade the media for a few months after Amutha's death. The issue could come up again. You cannot afford to spoil your name and the party's reputation. At least for the next few months be careful," Elangovan warned.

As Agathiyan was about to leave the room, Elangovan stopped him. "Wait. I am going to call the key members of our party next week and we need to discuss our strategy, including possible alliances. I will strongly push for your candidature again. You will contest from one of the three very strong constituencies where we have never lost ever since this party was formed. I am not keeping good health.

You and I have to set things up before anything happens to me..."

When Elangovan said this, Agathiyan interrupted, "Appa, don't talk like this... You will live a hundred years."

"Stupid fellow, this is not the time to be emotional. Show your emotions to the stupid public but exhibit logic and smart thinking internally. I am eighty-five with several health complications. Fuck! I am unable to even enjoy two whiskeys happily. I have to struggle hard even to urinate peacefully. Listen, don't go out of the city next week; let's call for the meeting. Karadi will also be there, I need to tackle him—you don't know his type!"

Elangovan continued, "From now on, get used to calling me 'Thalaivar', avoid addressing me as 'Appa'."

Agathiyan smiled.

"Now you can go. Also, henceforth get used to wearing our dhoti. Everyone should get the impression that you are seriously involved in the affairs of the party."

"Sure App... Sorry! Sure, Thalaivarae."

Elangovan smiled, despite his hurting, painful jaw.

* * * * *

KALPANA

"Hi Doctor, good morning! I wanted to tell you that I am feeling very good after the root canal. Thanks a lot." Kalpana received this long text from Suraj at around 10:00 PM. She was watching 'Money Heist' on Netflix, and though she was deeply engrossed in the exciting web series, she put it on pause mode and continued to chat with Suraj.

"Good to hear that. I was wondering why there was no feedback after you were crowned ten days back." Kalpana responded.

"Sorry about that! Yes, it is a great feeling to get crowned by a queen." Pat came the response from Suraj.

"Hmm, I don't qualify as a queen."

"Of course, you do. You are a smart, beautiful, accomplished, educated queen!" Suraj amplified the warmth in his message.

"You don't know about me. I should be doing better than what I am currently doing. I'm really stressed."

Suraj could sense that Kalpana had a story to narrate and a host of problems to share. He had two options: One was to divert the topic and arrest the flow without getting into the details. The other was to know more and be of some help to her. He did a quick assessment. He somehow liked Kalpana a lot. It was natural for any man to like her. Her height, complexion, style quotient, figure and body language were too appealing to be ignored. Suraj was keen to befriend her. He did not know her personal background. Neither was Kalpana aware of Suraj's background.

The delay in his response made Kalpana ponder over the message sent by her. For a moment she wondered if she should have just thanked him for the compliments and left it at that. It had been ages since she had gotten compliments from a worthy man. She picked up the remote and was about to continue with 'Money Heist' when a message popped up on her WhatsApp.

"Come on, there are ways to handle stress. All of us have stress. I can guide you if you are okay with it. I can recommend a few books as well." Suraj responded after a while. He didn't want to lose his connection with her.

"Thanks, Suraj. I am fine. Nothing major. Just some challenges in generating revenue. I guess I need to be patient." Kalpana responded, indicating clearly that the stress was just on account of business pressures.

"Oh Queen, order this Minister into your ministry, and I shall help you." The message, with its friendly and casual tone, instantly lightened her mood.

"Will do. Talk tomorrow, Minister."

"I am fine to talk now. After all this poor guy is single and not in demand." Suraj gave clear signals to Kalpana, and she quickly understood what he wanted to convey. That he was single and available.

"Hmm. Not now. Can't disturb my daughter. She is sleeping." Kalpana managed to convey that she was a mother already.

"Oh… No rush, Doc. We will talk tomorrow. Good night. Your hubby must be wondering what you are up to now!!!"

"No, that's not a problem. I am single. I don't know why I am sharing my personal info with you." This response from Kalpana boosted Suraj's mood. He got the message that she was somehow single. Perhaps she had separated from her husband or maybe her husband had died young. He was not bothered, and in reality, he felt a tad relieved, but obviously couldn't afford to exhibit his feelings.

"Sorry about that, K. Let's not text now, we will talk sometime later. Don't worry, I can be your sounding board," Suraj managed to send an emotional response.

"Thanks, Suraj. Really happy with your offer. Your professional expertise will be really helpful." Kalpana responded sincerely.

Suraj was a bit confused as he found her response ambiguous. He hoped his time wouldn't be used for professional consulting only. He had a different agenda.

"Of course, K. Anything for you."

'You are really sweet." Kalpana also responded sweetly.

The chat went on till 11:45 PM, and they finally decided to meet up for lunch in the next couple of days.

Suraj switched on his Smart TV to watch a movie. He picked up a pint of Hoegaarden beer and settled down comfortably on his couch, while Kalpana switched off her TV and crashed on the bed.

* * * * *

ELANGOVAN

That evening Elangovan specifically asked Agathiyan to stay at home. He invited three of his most trusted, senior party members who had been with him ever since the party was formed: Muthukaruppan, Pandiyan and Charumathi.

There were very strong rumours that Charumathi and Elangovan had been in a relationship in the past, and even had a daughter who had already been married off to another member of the party. Charumathi's affair with Elangovan was well known to her husband, but he had little to say as he had gained a lot in his business from Elangovan's political connections.

After Elangovan crossed fifty, the relationship gradually fizzled out though politically Charumathi retained Elangovan's confidence, trust and faith. She was sharp, bold and courageous, and hence she shone well in a male-dominated space.

The purpose of the meeting was to discuss strategies. Generally, what got approved and affirmed by this set of people became the party's stand as well. It was always easy for these powerful people to push their agenda amongst the others, and they had their own ways of silencing dissenters within the party.

Karadi Kathiresan was the only one among the seniors who wouldn't abide by their norms if they didn't favour his personal agenda. Yet, he was not that much of a worry as the majority of the members knew that the power was vested with Elangovan, Muthukaruppan, Pandiyan and Charumathi.

From 7:00 PM onwards, the members arrived one after the other. Normally, Elangovan held such confidential meetings in a well-equipped room that was adjacent to the large drawing room. While a meeting was on, no one would enter without prior consent. The windows of the room were soundproof, and the walls were also thick. Elangovan knew that walls had ears and he had carefully silenced them.

Once all of them arrived, Agathiyan made sure that they were received and led to the room. The room was carpeted wall to wall. A large table and a huge chair with leather upholstery were clearly reserved for the leader. There were several photographs, some on the walls, some on top of the wooden cabinet behind the table. The only common factor in all the photographs was Elangovan's presence.

There was one meeting table with eight chairs around them, a TV with a large screen, a refrigerator, a mini bar that had adequate stocks of liquor, and a bookshelf with biographies and books relating to politics.

As they continued to converse, Elangovan entered the room. He looked different in coloured clothes—a maroon T-shirt and lounge pants (his preferred style of dressing)—

and a tad younger too. He was comfortable in these compared to the pristine white shirt, dhoti and towel, an attire that served no purpose other than creating some visibility for his party flag through its border.

Everyone got up and wished him in the customary style with folded hands. In a chorus, they uttered, "Vanakam, Thalaivarae" (Hello, Chief).

"Welcome... hope all are fine?" Elangovan asked them to sit. He himself took longer to settle in his seat, as his weak spine always caused him pain in the back. Others took their seats around the large meeting table.

"What will you all have? These days I am unable to take more than one drink. The doctor has strictly advised me to stick to that." Agathiyan fetched a large whiskey on the rocks for his father.

Others also filled their glasses with whatever they wanted. When Charumathi hesitated, Elangovan urged her to feel comfortable. "At least have some wine, Charu," he suggested.

"Okay, Thalaivarae, I will have whiskey. I don't like wine." She poured herself a large and added water to the drink.

Agathiyan chose not to drink at that time.

Elangovan initiated the discussion "Look, I am not all that well and you know it. My spine, heart, lungs and kidneys are not in good condition. I don't know if I will live beyond a year. You need not become emotional about it. We all die someday. Considering my health and energy, I think I should not be the CM candidate, though we will not announce that immediately. I want you people to ensure Agathiyan gets chosen for the position. I promise I shall take care of all of you with good ministerial berths and I shall appoint one of you as Deputy CM, we can create even two Deputy CMs—which fucker can dare question us?"

He sipped his whiskey and relished the taste.

There was a hushed silence for a while. Pandiyan broke the silence. "Chief, we will certainly do it for you. Thambi (brother) Agathiyan is more than eligible. He is educated also and today's youth will welcome this decision. But you will always remain our Thalaivar."

"Thalaivarae, we will have to manage a few people within the party. Thambi lost the last election, hence there will be some questions. But I will manage them. We will have to silence the members supporting Karadi, and this can be managed with money. Anything for you Thalaivarae..." Pandiyan endorsed.

"What, Charu, you are silent?" Elangovan sought her opinion, knowing that she would have the right point of view.

"Thalaivarae, Thambi Agathiyan is our next CM, no doubt about that. But..." She hesitated and looked at all the others.

"Charu, this is amongst us. Whatever we discuss here is confidential and everyone has a right to speak openly. No one should misunderstand anyone. So, please go ahead and say whatever's on your mind." Elangovan gave her the green signal to share her opinion.

Charumathi continued after taking a large sip from her glass. "Public opinion has to be changed and manipulated. Amutha's death is still a mystery to the public, and the Opposition will use this as a ploy to pitch the women voters against Thambi. The relationship with Thambi's earlier girl, that dentist, will also be misused. You know very well how people create memes these days and tarnish the image of whoever they want. Some know that Thambi had an affair with that dentist, and the view is that Thambi ditched her and the daughter born to them." She then looked at the others. Agathiyan shifted nervously. She took another sip from her glass.

"Hmm... Charu, you are right. That's why I respect your views. But Charu, we have time—another eight to nine months—we can do something to improve Thambi's image." Elangovan then looked at Agathiyan. "Thambi, are you listening? We can make mistakes but we should have the ability to hide them or else we will be screwed. Henceforth be careful and listen to us."

"Certainly, Thalaivarae." Agathiyan just uttered two words and smiled at the others as a mark of thanks and happiness. He knew that someday he was going to be the CM.

"Thalaivarae, my suggestion is that you should be our CM and Thambi can be later inducted as Deputy CM. This would be a good start for Thambi," Charu concluded. Everyone nodded in agreement.

"Fine, all of you can continue to have drinks and discuss. Eat well before you leave. We will keep this in mind and manage our party accordingly. Muthu, pay some of the media people and try to get some good stories written on Agathiyan. Closer to the election, we will even get one or two TV channels to project him well. Charu, during the next four months, make sure that Thambi participates in many women's welfare programmes. Handle it properly; you will be the best one to do it. I am feeling tired; let me retire." Elangovan left, confident that his followers would lead the State after he ceased to exist.

By the time the others finished their drinks and left the place it was 11.30 PM.

* * * * *

SURAJ

Suraj was waiting for Kalpana at Taj Connemara. The initial decision of meeting just for a coffee had gotten converted into a lunch meeting. Suraj, as usual, looked dashing in a pristine white linen shirt and faded jeans. A camel brown belt enhanced the style quotient. He was clean-shaven, and he smelled great having splashed on Ambre Nuit from Christian Dior.

Suraj won many eyeballs while waiting for Kalpana, and he loved the attention. Just as he was about to call Kalpana, he saw her entering the lobby. Both of them started smiling at each other from a distance; both nursed an intense curiosity about each other.

"Hi, Suraj. Sorry if I kept you waiting," Kalpana tendered a not-so-serious apology.

"Not at all, K. I got here just ten minutes back." Suraj couldn't resist admiring her. Her silky hair was tied back in a neat ponytail. Her shapely body was clad in a black top and a knee-length leopard print skirt. Her shoes were stylish, yet comfortable, and added to her overall sophisticated look.

"K, you look beautiful. I genuinely feel you should have taken up modelling as a career. Have you ever thought about it?"

"Hmm... that's a long story. I would have done better as a model, perhaps!

Anyway, it is too late to regret my foray into this profession. I am committed to it. Considering the huge investments that I've already made, I can't reverse my decision now," Kalpana replied, with a flash of disappointment and concern on her clean and fresh face.

Suraj noticed it and was rather surprised that she had misunderstood his compliment. But he did infer that she was going through some financial hassles.

"Come on K, your profession should not stop you from getting into modelling. How can the beauty brands miss your endorsement? They are missing something major!" Suraj managed to set an easy tone and she guffawed on hearing his words.

They walked into 'Verandah', the restaurant. Suraj led her to the seats close to a glass window. The view was impressive and Kalpana's looks were enhanced by the natural light.

As they started on the hot soup, Suraj decided to lead the conversation. "Hey K, tell me more about yourself if you don't mind."

"What is there to mind, Suraj? Though I honestly don't know what made me accept this lunch meeting with you. We hardly know each other!" Kalpana raised a valid point.

"Do you regret this, K?" Suraj hoped fervently for a 'no' from Kalpana, and she replied likewise.

Kalpana then began to narrate her story, including personal details about how she got ditched, and how she started dental clinics not heeding her father's warnings on hypothecating the only property they had.

"Suraj, I have lost so far. But I want to win and win big time. I have to win for myself, for my daughter and for my father. I have the desire, and willingness to work hard, in fact, even slog, but I must win!" She laughed ruefully, "I don't know why I am sharing all these details with you. Perhaps I consider you a sounding board."

After she spoke, Suraj noticed that Kalpana's eyes had a fire in them. But along with that fire, there were tears as well. He empathized with her. He understood her pain and her resolve to become someone successful, prominent, wealthy and popular.

"You can do it, Kalpana, and you will do it. You have age on your side, and the fire within you. Rest assured, Kalpana, I shall support you throughout. I will be with you all along. You can count on my friendship for life." Suraj meant every word, and he clasped her hands as added assurance.

They continued to eat as they sipped their chilled beer which was very soothing in the hot and humid Chennai weather.

"How much have you invested so far, K?"

"For both clinics put together, around thirty-five lakhs. And the revenue I generate barely enables me to meet the overheads and some of my expenses. I'm not proud to say it, but that's a fact. I wonder if I should spend more on marketing..." Kalpana responded.

"Hmmm. Do you want to create more and more revenue over the long term? Or do you want to quickly become very wealthy?" Suraj surprised Kalpana with this question.

"If you ask me, Suraj, I want to become reasonably wealthy quickly. More importantly, I want to become powerful and prominent. I may be able to achieve all this with time. But I don't want to wait. I want it to happen soon. And I want to be able to enjoy my power and wealth before I get too old. Am I too greedy?" Kalpana winked as she sought a reply.

"Not at all. I love your clarity. Take it from me, you will become reasonably wealthy in less than one year, provided you follow my advice and trust me." Suraj's words showed Kalpana a ray of hope.

"I shall!" Kalpana gripped Suraj's hand. They were silent for a while and the silence spoke volumes, conveying and confirming many things to both of them.

They finished lunch, and Suraj checked if Kalpana wanted to go over to his apartment, but she said that she would rather do that on some other day. They hugged each other briefly at the lobby, and left the hotel, but not before Suraj promised to call her later to take the 'wealth creation' discussion forward.

After reaching their respective homes, Suraj texted: "Thanks K, for accepting my invite. I had a lovely time."

Kalpana responded: "Thanks S, I enjoyed myself too. Time well spent..."

"Oh, that's nice. We can now call ourselves KS." Suraj texted.

"Stands for what????????"

"Kama Sutra!" Suraj texted, and eagerly awaited her response, wondering if he had overstepped boundaries.

"Hmmm, interesting. You are too fast!" Kalpana added, "Bye for now, I have some work."

"Ha ha, I shall wait. I must tell you once again—you looked stunning today, dear. Bye for now." Suraj texted.

"You too looked dashing and stylish. But don't shave your face clean. You look better with a stubble. More later," Kalpana replied.

"Thanks, dear. Bye."

The conversation ended, and a new project for Suraj commenced.

* * * * *

MEENA

It was Sunday. Kalpana woke up a little later than usual that morning but still went through her routine of yoga and pranayama. She pampered herself on Sundays with an abridged version of yoga. Breakfast on Sundays was always ordered from Ratna Café, as her father just loved the taste of sambar from there.

Unless there was an emergency or an unavoidable patient, Kalpana did not open her clinics on Sundays. A few times she had evaluated the idea of opening the clinics for a few hours on Sundays, for extra revenue. However, her initial experiments yielded disappointing results. So, she decided to keep the clinics closed and enjoy her Sundays. On Sunday evenings, she preferred to hang out with her small group of friends.

There was another important task that she set aside for Sundays. She made it a point to spend some time with Meena and help with her studies. Though Meena was helping Kalpana at her clinic and also did some domestic chores at home, she was also pursuing her studies through distance learning. It was Kalpana's resolve to take care of Meena, who had been referred to her a few years ago by her friend.

Meena had a normal childhood till about fourteen, then something had happened that had traumatized her deeply. The real reason for the trauma was never known. Meena's father was happy that Meena was in good hands, getting proper care and shaping up well. Somehow, Meena had never revealed what had caused her trauma. For almost one year she suffered from severe depression and had to drop out of regular school. The doctor who was treating Meena knew Kalpana, and during one of their meetings at the doctor's clinic, Kalpana saw Meena and was moved by the plight of the young girl. Meena's cute, innocent face drew Kalpana towards her. She volunteered to take care of Meena. A meeting was arranged with Meena's father, who was only too happy that his only child was going to be taken care of.

Meena's entry into Kalpana's life also gave Kalpana additional purpose and a much-welcome diversion. Meena was also very helpful to Kalpana. She had grown into a beautiful young girl in the last few years on account of the better environment and care. She gained more confidence in communicating with people and managed to gradually overcome the emotional and psychological trauma. Kalpana had probed subtly to uncover the cause of her trauma, but Meena just turned pale and fell silent. Kalpana then tactfully changed the topic and diverted her attention.

Both of them then left home to pick up vegetables and groceries from a neighbourhood store. As they stepped out, Kalpana received a message: “Hi K, let’s meet next week, my plans are ready.” It was from Suraj.

“What plans?????” responded Kalpana as she got into the car.

“To make you wealthy.”

“Wow, that was quick. What next?” Kalpana was delighted.

“We will meet next week at your clinic,” Suraj suggested.

“Done deal. Shall ping you later. Bye for now.” Kalpana started the car.

* * * * *

ELANGOVAN

Elangovan had to be rushed to the hospital. He had fainted at home.

Fortunately, Agathiyan was home and he took him with the helper's support to the hospital that was just two kilometres away. He didn't want to call an ambulance as the hospital was close by. Besides, he didn't want to attract media attention.

Elangovan was immediately seen, first by doctors in the emergency ward and then, after he was moved to the regular ward, more than two specialists visited, including Elangovan's cardiologist. The doctors prescribed a few tests.

The cardiologist, Dr Krishnan, came out to meet Agathiyan. He conveyed that there were no major concerns and that it seemed once again to be an episode of bradycardia.

"Agathiyan, let your father stay in the hospital for two days; we need to observe him. I suspect he is not taking care of his health. Is he under stress?" Dr Krishnan enquired.

"I am not sure, Doctor. Maybe he is stressed due to the forthcoming Assembly elections."

"When is the election?"

"The date hasn't been announced yet, Doctor. We certainly have a few months more to go, as we have elections in two other States prior to our State."

"Okay, then he should take it easy. You should take care of his work from now onwards. He has told me a few times that he has to somehow win this election. He even told me that he wants to die as a CM," the doctor related.

"We will surely win, Doc. All strategies are in place. The Opposition has also begun to feel the heat. I shall certainly do my bit. And thanks a lot for your prompt attention and care," Agathiyan said with genuine gratitude.

"The pathological report will be ready between today and tomorrow. I hope there are no surprises. His heart is weak and is not pumping well enough. All the heavy smoking and late nights have wrecked his health. To make things worse, he has not been a very obedient patient. He is generally weak too. Anyway, let's wait for the report." Dr Krishnan continued, "Agathiyan, you must be prepared—anything can happen. He is not looking very good in any case."

Dr Krishnan was not only a cardiologist treating Elangovan, he was also a family friend and a well-wisher. They had known each other for over twenty years.

"Doc, I shall come again tomorrow to see you and Dad. To the media and the party members, I'll just mention that he has just come for a check-up and that his BP is a bit low. I don't want people disturbing him here."

Agathiyan left the hospital, knowing that his dad was in safe hands. As he came out, he saw several missed calls, all from party members. Muthukaruppan had called him ten times, followed by calls from Pandiyan and Charumathi. There was also a missed call from Vanita.

Despite the pressure and the situation, Agathiyan was tempted to return Vanita's call. But he decided against it, and called Muthukaruppan and Pandiyan and briefly updated them. They were at the party office, and so he instructed his driver to take him there.

To stay connected and not displease Vanita, he sent her a WhatsApp message that he would call her later.

After reaching the party office, Agathiyan briefed the three close party members about his father's health. He didn't disclose what the doctor had finally told him about his father not looking good.

"Thambi, Kathiresan wants to meet your father. Now that he has to take bed rest, I shall tell him that we will inform him later regarding the meeting," Muthukaruppan informed Agathiyan.

"Good. Let him wait... But why does he want to meet him? Just to wish him a quick recovery? I doubt if that's his only reason..." Agathiyan wondered.

"It can't be just that; he surely will have an agenda. Let's put him off." Muthukaruppan continued, "Take care of our Thalaivar, we will talk later."

Two days later, Elangovan was discharged from the hospital. He was brought home and was advised bed rest for a week. A few more medicines were added to the already long list. A medical support system was created at home, including the deployment of a nurse 24/7 to monitor Elangovan's pressure and pulse and to ensure he took all his medicines on time.

* * * * *

KALPANA

Kalpana was experiencing mixed feelings. On one hand, she was dismayed—it was a Tuesday and there was not a single appointment till 3:00 PM. On the other, she was elated about Suraj finding solutions to her problems.

The meeting with Suraj was confirmed and was expected to be a long meeting, with a practical, no-fuss business lunch to be delivered at the clinic. She was confident that Suraj was serious about making her wealthy, but she wasn't sure about the process, requirements, expectations and feasibility. She also wondered why he would do this for her. Yes, his interest in her was evident, and she was expecting this to lead to a relationship or, if nothing else, to a one-night stand.

She chose a simple, classy sleeveless pink top with a small floral print worn over slim-fit, ankle-length khaki pants. She left her hair loose and it flowed down to the middle of her back in shining, bouncy waves, framing her face softly. She applied a mild lipstick and splashed Burberry perfume on herself. A small gold chain with a tiny pendant adorned her long neck. She also applied an eyebrow enhancer for that added touch of elegance. She looked at herself in the mirror and was pleased with the reflection. Telling herself she could easily win the Miss Chennai title, she left for the clinic in high spirits.

At the clinic she felt rather restless. She prayed that she would get a good solution from Suraj. She was also aware of the attraction she felt. She was happy and excited when he was around. It was a pleasant feeling, a rush of blood she hadn't experienced since her relationship with Agathiyan.

Suraj entered. Immediately, the air in the consulting room seemed charged with his charm and energy. Suddenly, the room seemed brighter. The pace of Kalpana's heartbeat increased a notch.

He shook her hands and hugged her lightly. He believed that at times, rights have to be exercised without any need or silly wait for formal approval or confirmation. Kalpana loved not only the hug but also his lack of hesitation in claiming it as rightfully his.

Suraj had thoughtfully picked up a case of hot tea from the nearby Chai King outlet, and he carefully poured the tea into two cups. As they started sipping the tea, he began to narrate the business plan.

"Kalpana, listen to me carefully. It's good that you have created a private limited company for this business. Now, you are the main shareholder and you have given a few shares to your father, just for the sake of it. You have very little liability towards working capital, and assets mainly in the form of equipment, furnishings and rent advances.

See, the plan now is to buy, or lease, at least a hundred more clinics within the next three months. For now, we will limit ourselves to South India. Later, we will expand to the entire country. Does That sound interesting, K? Is it exciting you?" Suraj winked.

"What are you talking about? Are you drunk? There's hardly enough money to run these two clinics in the first place! And you want to buy a hundred clinics?" Kalpana was disappointed that Suraj was making a joke out of her goal to become rich and powerful. "Suraj, I thought you had some serious plans, I can't take this joke; it is not funny."

"My dear, dear, K! Damn it, I am serious. We will not stop with a hundred, we will reach five hundred, trust me. And don't worry about the money—the money will flow—leave that part to me, K." Suraj was serious when he said this.

He then explained the plan in detail. He picked up her prescription notepad and began to write in bullet points:

- Borrow to buy existing clinics and lease new clinics
- Infuse capital at a premium from angel investors
- Acquire 50-100 clinics
- Go for VC funding from my company
- Plan for 500 clinics
- Unlock value at an apt time

"Suraj, thanks for your prescription. I understood just 30% of what you said. Will this work? And will you handle all of it?"

"It will work. All you need to do is to exhibit the guts and the will to stay the course."

"Who will lend me the money? And how do we identify existing clinics?" Kalpana sought a little more clarity.

"We can identify some clinics that are at vantage locations but not doing well. Some of them will be run by old, near-retirement people, and we will have ways to get to other clinics on some basis. Leave all that to me."

"Hope we are not doing anything illegal. I don't want to drown myself in a shit pot," Kalpana said firmly.

"Everything will be perfectly legal and above board, no worries. Regarding lenders, I have sources who lend at low rates. They do expect part interest in cash though, but we can manage that."

"Hmm, let me trust you. But Suraj, why me? You could have done this for anyone right? And what's your interest in this?" Kalpana came to the core point.

"You. You and your welfare are my interests. My company manages a fund from Mauritius dedicated to the healthcare and wellness industry. We have raised a hundred million USD and we need to deploy it in the right manner. I can make it happen using my influence as a partner. Plus, I see potential for our entity to make money. When that happens, I will personally make a lot of money from it all. That's how it works."

He continued, "As for your 'Why me?"... Well, I don't go around meeting and dating too many dentists, do I?" He said it with such a serious, straight face that both of them burst out laughing.

"What is the timeline for all this to happen?" Kalpana again raised a valid point.

"It's time-bound, but you will make it for sure. As a matter of fact, your immediate cash flow issues will get resolved."

"Okay. What next?" Kalpana asked.

"We will order a quick bite... and let's hug one more time."

"There's no way I can say 'no' to that!"

They hugged, but this time the hug was much tighter. Suraj ran his fingers through her luxurious mane. He brought her face close to his and started kissing her passionately. Kalpana opened her mouth a bit and allowed Suraj to explore more with his tongue. Their tongues met, each trying to dominate the other. Kalpana started to moan. But when Suraj started kissing her naked shoulder, she stopped him.

"Suraj, this is my clinic. Some other time, please."

"You are irresistible, K. You taste great and smell amazing. This can't wait for long. Let's plan something soon." He once again kissed her passionately, and they moved away from each other.

They ordered pizza and after an hour Suraj left the place.

Kalpana was excited about her newfound partner, a partner not merely in business.

* * * * *

ELANGOVAN

After Elangovan had taken a few days' rest, Agathiyan informed him that Karadi Kathiresan had expressed his desire to meet him, preferably in private.

Elangovan, who was still confined to bed for most of the day, managed to take care of his routine to a great extent. His decibel level had reduced due to fatigue and medication. His speed of walking had also reduced.

"He can meet me any time after one week. I think it will be good for us to meet; he is a key person."

He then sat in his office room and directed Agathiyan to go to a small room attached to the master bedroom where there was a locker. "There will be a red-coloured file and a pen drive in the locker. Get them." He handed Agathiyan the keys to the locker. It was the first Agathiyan had heard of such a locker. He went to the room that was attached to the master bedroom. It would barely qualify as a room; it was just eighty square feet. Besides hundreds of shawls stacked in a wooden cupboard and gifts received during public functions arranged in one corner, there was a safe deposit locker. From the look of it, it appeared old.

After scanning the room, Agathiyan opened the locker. He expected to see bundles of cash, gold and precious stones—perhaps as a result of watching too many movies. Instead, he was in for a surprise. It contained several old photo albums and a few party-related documents. Below the stack of albums, he spotted the red-coloured file The pen drive was also there, tucked inside a tiny potli.

He wanted to open the file and check its contents immediately. But he controlled himself and took the file and the pen drive to his father's office room. Elangovan opened the file. There were just two sheets of paper inside it. He began explaining them to Agathiyan:

"Look, I don't know if something will happen to me..."

"Appa, don't talk like that..."

"Shut up. Just listen carefully."

On the first sheet, there were several names mentioned under the heading: 'Birthdays of Party members and families'. There were several names written with their birthdays and in some cases, their wedding dates too.

Pandiyan
Birthday: 28/08/1965
Wedding date: 08/ 12/ 1994
Muthukarrupan
Birthday: 14/10/1967
Wedding date: 02/05/1995
Saravanan: Birthday 06/06/1974
James: Birthday 12/05/1971

Similarly, there were several names with dates—some had both birthdays and wedding dates and some only wedding dates.

"Agathiyan, this file is important. Keep it safe, always."

Agathiyan found this a bit strange. "Appa, sorry to question you... but do you think these details are important enough to be kept in the locker? I find it really bizarre."

"Do you think your father is a crackpot? These are very important names and these people are very close to us. My intention is not to remember the birthdays of these people. Do I really care about that? I wish them on their birthdays anyway whenever my assistants remind me. The people listed here are the ones who have our money. They are our benamis. Some of them are rich on their own, as they have also swindled money at every opportunity. The month in their date of birth multiplied by twenty is the amount in crores that they are holding for us. The returns are anywhere between 0.5% to 1% in cash per month. Some don't pay anything as the money is reinvested in lands all over the State. Nearly 6000 crore rupees are invested in this manner. You can total it up and check.

Some of them have used this money to invest in businesses and some lend money to others. Since we get the interest in cash and nothing is disclosed including the capital, the rate of interest is low. But, let me tell you, these people won't cheat us. Not because they are noble souls, but because they are shit scared of me."

"Wow, Appa! This is good. But I think you are worth more and this is just a portion of the whole." Agathiyan was gaining interest.

"Of course, what do you think of your father? Today, even an ordinary MLA makes tons of money in five years," Elangovan grinned.

He then moved towards another wooden cupboard. Opening one of the drawers, he picked up a steel box. He brought it to Agathiyan and opened the box. In it were some visiting cards and three old keys. He picked up one key and showed it to his son.

"This is the key to a locker in HDFC Bank. I will soon nominate you as an authorized person to operate it. There is nothing in this locker except a few more keys, and each of those keys is a key to a safe deposit locker in different banks. All the documents pertaining to our commercial buildings, landed properties, residential villas and apartments, and even gold and other jewellery are kept in these lockers. Some of them are disclosed assets but many are not.

I will also give you the contact details of two financial advisors, Chandrasekhar in Chennai, and Naveen Gupta in Mumbai. I will introduce you to these two over the phone; they are very smart guys. They manage our overseas investments..."

Even before Elangovan could complete the sentence, Agathiyan intervened "Overseas? You mean we have commercial and residential properties in other countries?"

"No, no. Through hawala, we have routed the money to some venture capitalists and private equity firms. Chandrasekhar and Naveen are experts in this. You must understand that this same money comes back to India as investments in start-ups, and we make tons of money from this. These firms are in Mauritius and Curaçao. We own a major share in some of them. The amount invested is well over eight hundred crores. And, of course, we have official and declared investments in many companies as well."

The grin on Elangovan's face widened. "Appa how did you manage to do so well and build wealth? We must be worth more than two thousand five hundred crores." Agathiyan's curiosity mounted.

"Fool, we are worth over fifteen thousand crores, I shall share other details with you later, one bit at a time. You should start getting more involved now. I am also a partner in the business run by our Muthukaruppan and Pandiyan, I will share the details later."

"Sure, Appa. I know you bought a small villa too, in Kodaikanal. This was when Amma was still alive, years back. I hope you still have it." Agathiyan wanted to impress his father by proving to him that he remembered an asset bought by his father a long time ago.

"Ah, not bad, you remember it. I gave it off to Sarasu, that actress who used to act in movies those days."

"Why Appa? You sold it or you just donated it?"

"I gifted it to her. She used to take care of your dad whenever he felt stressed and tired ..." A snide smile conveyed the message and Agathiyan was neither surprised nor disappointed. In fact, he was rather proud of his father.

* * * * *

SURAJ

"Darling, what's up? Shall we meet again today?" It was Suraj's message to Kalpana. There had been no communication from him in the last ten days.

Instead of responding to the message, Kalpana called him instantly. "Hello, big man! No news from you for the last ten days, and now I am suddenly your darling?" Kalpana spoke in mock anger.

"I told you earlier, and let me tell you again, I was working only for you, on your project. And—I have some good news." Suraj kindled Kalpana's curiosity.

"Really? Oh, tell me, tell me! I need to go to the clinic, there are four appointments this morning."

"Only when we meet this afternoon. And all the details when you come home in the evening. Come prepared, you can leave at night from here."

"This seems to be an offer I can't refuse, though I can perhaps resist it," Kalpana teased him.

"As you wish, K." Suraj was confident that Kalpana would yield to the offer.

"It all depends upon the update that you intend to share with me this afternoon. Come after 4:00 PM," Kalpana countered.

"Done, darling. Bye for now."

By 4:30 PM Kalpana was through with work. It had been a good day for her. She had secured three new patients. One of them had many complications that needed treatment for a longer period, ensuring more revenue in the days to come.

Kalpana was contemplating whether or not to call Suraj, when he arrived with a cake.

"Let's first cut the cake." He started to unbox the cake.

"Occasion?" Kalpana was indeed excited but wanted to know the reason nevertheless.

"K Clinic is in expansion mode." As he said this, he lit the tiny red candle on the cake and asked her to blow it. They cut it together, and fed slices to each other. Suraj smeared some cream from the cake on her cheeks and licked it off them.

He whispered into her ear, "I need to apply this cream all over you." Kalpana was thrilled. She blushed and pushed him away half-heartedly.

Suraj then started his narrative. "I have arranged for funds, both in the form of equity and some low-cost debt. Our company will also invest at an appropriate time. We shall rebrand your clinic as K Clinic, and we will change the name of the company to K Clinic Lab. The word 'lab' works some magic in the stock market, and the letter K will do bigger magic, you just wait and see."

He winked at her and continued, "K Clinic Lab will get a reasonable amount of money through borrowings and angel investors, and you will continue to hold over 75% of the company. I have already identified twenty dental clinics to be acquired in Chennai and a further three each in Coimbatore, Madurai, Trichy and Pondicherry. This is just the start. Within the next forty-five days, we shall identify twenty more in our State, and some more in the other Southern States. In the next two months or so, there will be one hundred clinics. If we need money, we can always get it from other angels. Some of these clinics we won't buy but we will run them under our banner. After you build 100 plus clinics, Green Stream will enter and take K Clinics to a 500-plus chain."

He paused for breath and asked how it all sounded.

"My God, all this sounds too amazing to be true! But I can't clearly understand the process you are explaining. I am not good with numbers and finance. I hope the path is legal. It is, isn't it, Suraj?

"Darling, I am going to be involved too. This is legal, no worries at all, trust me!"

"How come so many people agreed to sell? Or even allow us to operate their clinics under our banner?" Kalpana raised a point.

"See, some are not doing well but enjoy prime locations. They are run by old people who are not marketing savvy. Hence, they are keen on selling and they are prepared to let us run the units in the manner we want. Some who don't want to sell, are willing to run their clinics under our banner provided they get something out of it. I will manage all this... I have a team working on it. It is just a matter of time before one gets to see K Clinic Labs all over the State and region."

"Suraj, I can't visualise this. But if it happens, I will be eternally grateful to you. I want to make it big in life, make money and have power. The fall in my life has taken its toll on me and..."

Suraj hushed her by placing his fingers on her lips. He took her hand and noticed how beautifully she had shaped her nails. He loved the fact that the thumbnail had a different colour of nail polish than the other nails.

"Just don't get emotional. Your bitter past is over. Together we will create a great future for ourselves. You focus on scaling the teeth of your patients, while I'll help you in scaling up your business." He kissed her hand tenderly.

"But tell me, how will we generate income from these clinics? There should be enough return on our investment, right?"

"Not bad, K, you are now talking like a finance professional. Good question. Well, we will generate revenues from various sources. We will market big time, very aggressively. We will get Government contracts where we will do oral health check-ups at all Government schools. Of course, the Health Minister will become richer and will have a bigger paunch," Suraj laughed as he continued. "We will tie up with one or two large companies in the oral health space, and by giving them enough publicity and visibility at all our centres, we will create another revenue stream. This is just the beginning. Oh...and we need to hire an actress who will be our brand ambassador."

"You mean one with great teeth?" Kalpana was excited.

"Maybe, yes, but more importantly someone with a hot figure, who is the heartthrob of the masses."

Both laughed.

"And, K, I shall share other plans this evening at my place. I have to meet someone now, I shall pick you up at 7:00 sharp. I hope our plan still stands?"

"Yes, dear, it is on... but I need to be back home by 10:00 PM latest."

"Oh, sure." He got up and, before leaving the place, planted his face on her neck and painted her neck with his nose and lips. He then kissed her wildly before tearing himself away.

Kalpana had started enjoying every moment with him. Every step forward with him helped her move on from where Agathiyan had left her all alone.

She couldn't wait for 7:00 PM, to get picked up by Suraj. She knew Meena would take care of her little daughter at home.

* * * * *

THE PARTY MEMBERS

Pandiyan had blocked a room in his own four-star hotel in Vadapalani. He normally used this room to discuss political issues with his close aides, including Muthukaruppan, and sometimes Charumathi. At times, he also used this suite to entertain bureaucrats with wine and women, as confidentiality was assured.

Everything had been arranged, including Pandiyan's favourite Old Monk Rum. Despite being able to afford the most expensive liquor, Pandiyan always opted for Old Monk. Whenever he was served single malt whiskey, he used to share his disdain for the drink with his friends. He wondered why people paid so much for a bottle.

Muthukaruppan arrived and went straight up to room 501 where they usually met. Pandiyan and he had been friends for many years now and had come up together in the political echelon. In the past, they had held the position of MLAs. Despite belonging to different castes, they bonded very well.

Pandiyan was elder to Muthukaruppan who addressed him as 'Annae' (elder brother). While they maintained the needed diplomacy when others were around or in public, they shared a deep personal bond in private, one-to-one meetings. They shared many secrets, and both were extremely loyal to Elangovan.

After downing two quick pegs, Pandiyan asked Muthu if he knew why Kathiresan wanted to meet Elangovan in private and whether it would have any political implications.

"Annae, don't worry. It could be a good thing. Kathiresan must have also realized that he has to align very well with Thalaivar."

"Muthu, I'm not sure. I hope Thalaivar doesn't make any rash promises. I have been in the ministry for a long time now, and I should rightfully be given the position I deserve. I have slogged like a dog and eaten shit like a pig to stay relevant in politics. You know that very well. If Kathiresan tries to fuck me, he will see another side of me." Pandiyan lit a cigarette and downed the third peg, anxiety and anger evident on his face.

"Don't worry, Annae. Nothing of the sort will happen. Thalaivar knows your strengths and Kathiresan's weaknesses. He will not take any decision without seeking our advice."

Pandiyan was rather relieved to hear this, and the meeting continued till late.

* * * * *

SURAJ

Suraj was late by fifteen minutes. Kalpana was just winding up, attending to the customary clear-up of her work desk. She was very particular about tidiness, and that was apparent in the way she maintained her home, her car, her office and even herself.

She got into Suraj's BMW 6 Series car, thinking to herself that someday she would also own such a car. The music was on, and Ed Sheeran was, in a way, obstructing the conversation between them. Suraj lived in the posh Boat Club area. He was the proud owner of a beautiful villa that he had bought a few years back by taking a sizeable home loan. He had always wanted to live in a very good property with an upmarket address. Suraj, being a successful professional, had another villa on the East Coast Road, one that he sometimes used to unwind in with his friends. Though he was thirty-five, he had remained single. He had never been in a serious relationship though he did have a few flings with women of his choice.

They reached the villa in good time as it was not far from her clinic. Ed Sheeran was cut off before he completed 'Shivers' from his album, Equals.

Suraj parked his car on the porch and gallantly held the door open for Kalpana. "A warm welcome to the princess," he said dramatically as he took her hand and led her to the main door. He used his keys to open the door, and Kalpana realized that he was alone in the house, without even a live-in domestic help.

The house was surrounded by a beautiful, well-maintained garden with many colourful flowering plants. The garden was a mood uplifter. The red tiles on the veranda that led to the main door appealed to Kalpana. She could see that Suraj had great taste.

When she entered the house, she was impressed by the large paintings occupying many parts of the wall in the living room. There was very little furniture in true minimalistic style, but everything was made out of high-quality teak. Kalpana fell in love with the house.

"You have a beautiful house, Suraj. And you do have exquisite taste," she remarked as she looked around.

"Thanks, K. Unless I had good taste, I wouldn't have fallen for this princess," Suraj complimented her. "Let me have a shower. You can use the other room to freshen up unless you want to shower with me," Suraj teased.

"Oh, get lost... I shall use the other room." Kalpana went into one of the two bedrooms on the ground floor while Suraj went up to the first floor.

"Come up to the first floor once you are through. I shall be eagerly waiting for you." Suraj winked at her as he climbed the spiral staircase from the large living room to the first floor.

Kalpana enjoyed her shower. The lukewarm water caressed and refreshed her. She felt a mix of anticipation, excitement and anxiety. She had not been out with a man since Agathiyan, and she sensed that the evening was going to be very different. She wanted it but felt a nagging sense of fear and guilt, one that almost obstructed her willingness to yield to temptation.

She came out of the bathroom and put on the dress she had brought—a simple yellow kurti and white leggings. She let her hair loose and examined herself critically in the big mirror in the bedroom. She loved the way she looked. She went to the first floor and saw Suraj filling two glasses with wine. The first floor housed a home theatre, a minibar, a small kitchen and a bedroom. Suraj was in a black Polo and denim shorts. His damp, tousled locks enhanced his cool looks.

When she went near him, he hugged her and planted a kiss on her cheeks and then on her long neck. His eager hands caressed her back.

"You smell so good, K."

"As do you," Kalpana responded as she hugged him tight. "Suraj, why don't you explain how the entire model works, our expansion programme, funds for the same, valuation ..." Before she could complete the sentence, Suraj grabbed her again and kissed her passionately. His grip became tighter, and his breath, warmer than before.

"K, all of that can wait. Now, let's just enjoy the evening."

Kalpana enjoyed his every touch. She loved his wild kisses. She found herself surrendering to his touch, melting in his arms. She had missed a man's touch all these years.

"But tell me, why me? I am sure there are many others you could have helped," Kalpana persisted.

"Yeah, but the first day I met you I fell for you and trust me, I am not exploiting your situation. You are irresistible to me in so many ways, dear."

Kalpana couldn't hold back her excitement and happiness when he said this.

The hugs continued and the wine bottle grew poorer in content. The kisses continued, their hands searched and felt each other everywhere, and the clothes came off their bodies. They lay completely naked on the bed exploring each other and savouring their togetherness. They made love to each other twice in quick succession and both relished the time they spent in bed together. Not much was spoken, except for a few whispers, in the last ninety minutes.

They were still in bed, with Kalpana resting her cheeks on Suraj's chest. "Suraj, what kind of relationship are we getting into?"

"We love each other and that's evident; we want each other, that's natural. Let's not ruin it by trying to define this relationship with a name," Suraj responded as he braided her hair.

"Meaning?" Kalpana wanted clarity.

"We will continue to be special friends, dear." He pulled her close and kissed her tenderly. "Let us not complicate our lives."

Kalpana understood. It was too early for commitment. When she sneaked a peak at her mobile phone which had been in silent mode for the last ninety minutes. She saw that it was already 10:30 PM. She got dressed and called for an Uber.

"I will drop you, K," he offered.

"No driving after three glasses of wine please," Kalpana was firm.

When the cab arrived, she hugged him once again.

"K, we have to discuss business next week. Let's meet at my office. Bye for now, and call me tomorrow, sweet."

"Sure, and thanks for a beautiful time."

"Thanks for your special friendship," Suraj responded.

Kalpana got into the cab and realized that there were four missed calls from her father. She called him to let him know that she was on her way.

She began to text Suraj: "Why am I special? Why do you like me?" Kalpana was curious and perhaps, fishing for compliments.

"You have the amazing qualities of a man and a woman." Suraj's response further kindled her curiosity.

"Meaning?"

"You think like a man—I just love your aspirations and drive, your anger, your resolve to prove a point. And you prove to be a woman with your grace, style, ability to handle stress and more importantly, enslaving my manhood. You are just amazing in bed. I surrender!"

Suraj responded in detail knowing that Kalpana would blush. And she did.

* * * * *

ELANGOVAN

It was an unusual time for Elangovan to meet anyone at home. He had invited Kathiresan over at 6:00 AM. Elangovan wanted to avoid unnecessary attention, even from his own party colleagues. An uneasy relationship prevailed between Elangovan and Kathiresan on account of the latter being disappointed on several grounds. Elangovan agreed to meet Kathiresan as he knew that he needed everyone's support to regain power.

At 6:00 AM sharp, security guards opened the huge gates to a white Innova after checking the car number and without asking any questions.

Kathiresan was visiting Elangovan at the latter's residence after many years. He had mixed feelings; he was not sure as to how he would be received and how the conversation would proceed. He held a large bouquet and carried a shawl with him. Nobody accompanied him as the plan was to have a free and open confidential discussion with Elangovan.

As he entered the large drawing room, Elangovan walked towards Kathiresan a little more briskly than he usually did. The men embraced; the hug conveyed a strong message of bonding which was perhaps natural, or perhaps forced by circumstances.

Kathiresan was hugely relieved at this warm reception.

He offered the bouquet to Elangovan and presented the shawl. "Aiyya (Chief), shall we take a picture with the bouquet and shawl? It may come in handy to circulate." Kathiresan checked if someone was around to take the picture.

"No, no! Let's not do that, Kathir. I am not wearing my customary white shirt and dhoti; it will not look appropriate. Many don't realize that I am sick of the same dress code. I wish someone would change it soon." Both laughed and the atmosphere became even more cordial.

"Where is Thambi Agathiyan?" enquired Kathiresan.

"He must be either sleeping or at the gym. He knows that we are meeting; I specifically told him to stay away. He will see you before you leave. Come, let's go to my room."

Kathiresan was glad that Elangovan had chosen not to have even Agathiyan around. They settled down in the room and soon piping hot filter coffee was served to them.

"Aiyya, thank you very much for magnanimously agreeing to meet me, especially with no one else around. Special thanks for such a warm reception from you."

"Come on Kathir, we have been together for many years now. We have travelled several highs and lows together. It's just that you chose to keep aloof from me. I do realize that you may have been disappointed with me sometimes..."

Elangovan's genuine warmth further boosted Kathiresan's morale.

"Nothing like that, Aiyya. I always knew that you would do something for me and my family members at the appropriate time. It is just that a few jobless people have been trying to create a rift between us by playing the caste card." Kathiresan subtly conveyed that the time had come for his elevation and the need for a roadmap for his grown-up children. Two of his three children were actively vying to move up the ladder rather than remain mere party members. Elangovan was sharp enough to understand the message, and also the reference to the caste card. He knew that it was Kathiresan's ploy to split the party on caste lines and make himself a force to reckon with within the party cadres. In politics, money power, religion, caste and vote share are the dominant decision-making tools.

"Kathir, our time has come, and so has yours. We have to crush the Opposition and erase them from the political scene. Our flag should fly high for the next few years, Kathir, even after my death. But I should die as the Chief Minister." The topic was gaining momentum.

"Aiyya, I am totally with you on this and I shall work for this tirelessly. But what's in store for me?" Kathir came to the point directly.

"Kathir, I will give you an important ministry. You take either Health or Home. I know many will resent my allotting this to you, but that's my promise."

"Aiyya, I am very grateful for this, but what about Muthu and Pandiyan? You should not change your mind tomorrow."

"I know, Kathir, they are very close to me and very important people too. I shall make one of them my Deputy CM and give either Home or Health to the other based on what you want to take. Are you happy?" Elangovan pushed to conclude the deal. He knew he could manage Muthu and Pandiyan.

"Definitely, Aiyya, I am happy. I would also like some say on seat allocation. My caste should have a decent amount of representation. I need to play this card for my benefit as well as for our party to triumph with the electorate."

"We will discuss that later, Kathir. You can trust me on it. And what I give to Pandiyan and Muthu will be my call." Elangovan was desperate but didn't want to show it.

"Aiyya, why do you think I won't trust you? Please take care of your health too."

"That reminds me...if anything happens to me before the election, Agathiyan should be the CM candidate. Mind you, I will not compromise on this."

Kathiresan was expecting this from Elangovan. "Absolutely, where is the doubt...but Aiyya..."

"Tell me, why the fuck this hesitation?" Elangovan was getting a tad restless.

“Nothing should happen to you, Aiyya… The thing is, Agathiyan Thambi’s reputation is no good. People are still talking about the mysterious death of his wife, and also his affair with that tooth doctor… What do they call such a doctor?”

“Dentist,” Elangovan responded tersely.

“Yes, that dentist. People are aware of how she was ditched and that she has a girl child through him. Aiyya, this is okay between us but during elections you know how the Opposition will rip us with it and use memes and media to leverage this subject in their favour.”

“I agree… What can we do to protect Agathiyan’s interest?” Elangovan sought Kathiresan’s views as he lit a cigarette. Despite strict advice from doctors, Elangovan continued to smoke once in a while, when he did not have too many people around him.

“Aiyya, it is better that they marry. That will boost his image among the emotional womenfolk.”

“Will that work? Will that dentist oblige?”

“Aiyya, we can get this done—a marriage of convenience only. My wife’s cousin is known to both Agathiyan and that dentist. She also studied in the same college. She is reasonably close to the dentist. I can ask her to broach the subject. After all, it is going to mean a redeemed life for her and her daughter as well. I will act on this if you permit me.”

Kathiresan's point of view seemed right to Elangovan. "Okay. Go ahead, Kathir. For now, don't discuss this topic with anyone else. And keep me updated."

The meeting concluded. Before Kathiresan left, Elangovan handed him a small bag filled with hard cash. "This is for our growing relationship, take it, Kathir."

Kathir accepted it without hesitation. In politics, nothing comes free. As he was about to leave, Agathiyan was called. They exchanged a few words and Kathiresan was sent off.

Elangovan, though relieved that his meeting with Kathiresan had gone well, was a bit worried about how the dentist would react. He knew he could easily manage Agathiyan.

* * * * *

ELANGOVAN

The date for the State Assembly elections was announced. There were just six months to go. Every media channel began focussing on the upcoming election. Speculation was rife as to who would align with whom, which politicians were to be watched, and how the central power would deal with the regional parties. There were meaningless, heated debates on every channel. There was also speculation that a few celebrities from the world of cinema and sports would either float their own parties or join some prominent ones. Political posts began trending on social media. Erstwhile friends on social media showed fierce political differences.

Meanwhile, Muthukaruppan and Pandiyan got the news that Kathiresan had met Elangovan and that they had spent quality time together. Elangovan hadn't updated Muthu and Pandiyan, and the latter was worried about it. He was growing hungry for power and position. He feared that Kathiresan would be a stumbling block to his ambitions. He was not on good terms with Kathiresan. Several things were responsible for this including previous disagreements, exchanges involving insults, filthy words and accusations, and, of course, caste issues.

Pandiyan and Muthu decided to gate-crash Elangovan's office. They had a good excuse: the announcement of the election date. The agenda was to have a preliminary discussion on strategy for the next few days. The hidden agenda was to uncover the outcome of the meeting between Elangovan and Kathiresan.

"Come ... come... I was about to call you. I didn't expect this date for the election. Even Praveen Sharma didn't give me any indication when I spoke to him about it last month." Praveen Sharma held a prominent post in the office of the Election Commission, and Elangovan had access to him.

"In a way it is good, Thalaivarae. The mood in the cadre is upbeat. The kind of mess the ruling party has created in the last few months will definitely work in our favour," Pandiyan opined.

"I agree. Let's get prepared. Shall we meet this Saturday? We can also call the other members of our core team," Elangovan suggested.

"Certainly. We were about to propose the same," quipped Muthukaruppan. "Thalaivarae, we heard that Kathiresan met you and we thought you would update us. You have to be careful with him," Muthu initiated the core subject.

"I know both of you are worried, I should have updated you. You have been in politics for many years and I am sure you understand that there has to be some give and take. We will be screwed right royally if we bother too much about ego. We can talk anything, but we need to be tactful in our dealings." As Elangovan explained,

Pandiyan and Muthu listened keenly but found this statement too airy.

"Thalaivarae, what are you trying to say? Sorry, we are unable to comprehend," Pandiyan said bluntly.

"See, he has been in our party for many years; he is becoming a power centre now. He has many friends in the Opposition party too, and we know it. He wants to ensure that he gets something worthwhile this time for sticking with us. Mind you, we also need him. Remember, his caste constitutes over twelve per cent of our State population and they are caste fanatics... just like most of us."

"So... what is it that you are promising him?" Pandiyan was a little anxious.

"I have offered him Home or Health when we win. And we are winning!" Elangovan clarified.

"But... Frankly, Thalaivarae, I thought I would get Home. I can't take anything less than what he gets." Pandiyan was forthright with his opinion and Elangovan sensed that he was perturbed.

"Pandiyan, I have something bigger for you. You think I will not consider your welfare? Is that the extent of our friendship and relationship? Apart from a good portfolio, I will assign a key role to you in party affairs. You will always be my second in command—that's my promise to you. Shed your hatred for Kathir now. We need him; if we lose him, we will get thrashed. And he can be nasty. Muthu, you will be given a very good portfolio, and as usual, a prominent position in the party too."

When Elangovan concluded, there were smiles all around. Pandiyan and Muthu were relieved.

"Let's show these guys who we are. We will spend as much as we can and bring out a manifesto that will lure the masses. Let's focus on getting the best media coverage. I will connect you people with Patrick who is an expert on this subject. Let him meet us and present his ideas later. He is sharp and effective and for us, he will charge a little more. Don't worry about spending; we should treat this as an investment. We will all reap the benefits for the next fifteen years. What do you say?" Elangovan looked at his team.

"We will do it! We will kill the Opposition! We will show our capabilities and what we are made of, Thalaivarae!" said Pandiyan, and Muthu acknowledged this by nodding vigorously.

The meeting ended with a plan to meet with the core team to strategize and finalize all action points before a general body meeting was called.

Muthukaruppan and Pandiyan left the place confident, happy and excited. Elangovan dialled Kathiresan's number. "Kathir, I hope that your wife's cousin will be meeting that dentist soon."

* * * * *

SURAJ

"Darling, I'll meet you at noon. Let's spend a couple of hours. I hope you don't have any patients scheduled at that time?"

Kalpana saw Suraj's message and responded: "I am tied up only from 4 to 7:00 PM. 12 to 2:00 PM suits me, baby."

"Meaning after 7:00 PM you are free." Suraj was fishing for an opportunity.

"Not today. Soon though... on my birthday, exactly six days from now."

"Great! Looking forward to it. Let's celebrate this special birthday in a special way." Suraj amped up Kalpana's expectations.

Kalpana knew that Suraj would arrive at her clinic at noon sharp. She had some work in the bank that morning. She completed it and got to her clinic by 11:00 AM. She had to handle scaling for a patient. She had a tough time doing it as it was the first time the patient was getting his teeth scaled in sixty years. His teeth were in a pretty bad condition. Kalpana, once in a while, regretted being a dentist and this was one such occasion. She charged him twenty per cent more, and the patient paid without complaint.

It was 11:45 AM when she completed her task and washed her hands. As usual, she freshened up with a face wash. At sharp noon, Suraj turned up.

Both were happy and excited to meet each other after a brief gap.

"Darling, I have some good news. I have lined up a few investors, and you will be out of your debts in just a few days. Not only that, we have identified clinics in Chennai and in several of the other Southern States, barring Kerala, for now. Very soon, there will be over thirty K Clinics. And this is just a start, dear."

Kalpana's eyes instantly filled with tears of joy, and she couldn't control her emotions. "Baby, tell me, how?"

"You may not understand much, but leave it to me to manage. In the next two months, you will have the largest network of dental clinics in the State."

"I trust you, Suraj... And how will I repay you for your services?"

"I have told you this earlier; I will be making money out of this too, as my own company will be investing soon as venture capitalists. Don't feel obligated at all, darling." Suraj held her hands.

"Okay, explain now." Kalpana got into a business discussion without diverting her attention and focus.

Suraj opened his Mac and quickly extracted an Excel sheet. He tried to explain to her in as simple a way as possible. He shared with her details of who would be investing, her initial dilution, settlement of the current working capital loan, etc. He also explained how they'd be buying some clinics, leasing some, and signing some up as franchisees. He explained that once all this was done, her clinic would have enough working capital, she would be debt-free, and would make over one crore for herself by diluting her stake.

Kalpana understood only thirty per cent of what he said but was filled with glee. She couldn't believe that this was happening to her.

"How are you so sure that this will work, Suraj? Sorry, I do trust you, but I am a bit scared to set my expectations."

"Let me explain briefly: there are a few investors who will invest now; they normally go by my word. The risk is not high, as they invest just a few lakhs each. For this, they get some equity. We leverage this money and borrow some more from larger institutions to increase our corpus. With this, we buy a few clinics and acquire many more, through leasing, franchising and other arrangements. We also spend a good sum of money on branding and marketing to increase our visibility. Revenues will start flowing."

Kalpana interrupted him, "But who will invest in clinics that are not profitable?"

"Scale dear, it is all about scale. It is all about storytelling with some data to back it up. If you focus on the profits of individual clinics, you don't cannot scale up. So instead, scale up and spin a story that wows investors."

"I know about only scaling of teeth." When Kalpana said this, they both laughed.

Suraj was lost in admiration of Kalpana's beauty. Her laughter enhanced the glow on her face, and her large expressive eyes sparkled more. Any day she was more attractive than the most colourful Excel sheet, and Suraj knew that.

Kalpana realized that Suraj's focus was shifting, and though she loved the attention, she tapped Suraj's hand. "Hello, Mr Suraj. Please stay focussed on the subject," she said, pointing her finger at the laptop. "This other matter is for some other time." The aroma of romance, love and lust permeated her not-too-big consulting room.

"See, Kalpana, you have some history of performance, and the ability to run your clinics. Hence, we can use that sensibly. We will also hire professional management, marketing and accounting teams, etc. As we keep expanding, And after we have a few more clinics in our kitty, our company can fund more and with that, we will expand to many other cities in the country. Later, we will go for a series of funding as we keep expanding, and someday, we either sell the business or just monetize in other ways, possibly a public issue too. K, I will keep teaching, mentoring and guiding you at every stage; no worries. You have to focus on building your personal brand... keep talking at various forums. I shall put you in touch with a few media people. Get as much visibility as possible—it will help." Suraj's briefing gave Kalpana a lot of confidence, and she decided that she would just follow Suraj's advice.

"And mind you, we will also create some fake revenues across the clinic using dummy names. We will generate fake revenues in cash and the source of that cash will be from a few who want to convert their black money into white. A significant portion of the cash received will be paid officially to their entities under some relevant heads of expenses. What we get is top line and some margins as well. All this will tide us over till we genuinely build revenues. You will know how it works as it spins out over time, but we will do it quickly. Once you consolidate, and later exit, we need to think of our next business. In the process, you can become a serial entrepreneur." The more Suraj explained, the more Kalpana's excitement scaled up!

"You mean to say that this will excite the investors—just increasing the number of clinics?"

"We will add stories like getting technology into this space and disrupting the industry. Technology and digitization will enable us to go global..."

Kalpana intervened, "Enough ... enough for the day, Suraj. Let me not get into a dream world now with a no-return option."

"In short, you will have more than a hundred crores within the next two years, or a little less if you opt to sell earlier. Hope that's good enough for you to start your next venture?" Suraj winked, and Kalpana couldn't resist hugging him. The hug naturally led to passionate kissing.

Being aware that the clinic was not a safe place for their capers, Kalpana got rid of Suraj half-heartedly, and asked, "Just tell me this – how do you create such believable stories for your investors?"

"I go with some researched data, some hypotheses, and fill numbers in an Excel sheet. And, voila! They ejaculate the story. I don't need to do anything else."

"How come?" Kalpana persisted.

"Just like I do when I am inside you. It is as natural as that."

Both laughed loudly.

* * * * *

KALPANA

Kalpana was getting ready with renewed energy. She realized that suddenly her fortunes were looking up, and her growing relationship with Suraj would be paying rich dividends.

"Kalpa, you seem very happy these days... anything special? Is your practice picking up or something? Please ensure you close the loan and release the property. You know how emotionally attached I am to this house." Kalpana's father could see that she was happy of late. He addressed her as 'Kalpa' when the mood was good.

Kalpana smiled, and she bent down to take her father's hand. "Appa, you are right, I am very happy these days. Business prospects are looking very bright, and within four to five months, the property will be released by the bank. Don't worry. I too am emotionally attached to this property. I can never forget the best part of my life that I have spent here when Amma was alive." When Kalpana said this, her father's eyes welled with joyful tears.

He blessed his daughter, "I wish you have a happy life, Kalpa. I pray you get married again to a nice man. One who will understand you and take care of you and your child—that's my only concern."

"Don't fret, Appa. Henceforth, life will be good for all of us."

Kalpana was not certain if her father sensed she was dating Suraj. She didn't want to probe too deeply. Meena watched them from afar with a rare smile on her face. Kalpana realized that it had been a long time since Meena had visited home and spent time with her father. Only when one goes through an experience can one have an idea of how it is for others going through something similar. Kalpana decided to send Meena to her place for a couple of days when she could manage her daughter's care by herself. Perhaps she'd choose a weekend when there were no plans with Suraj.

As she was about to leave, she received a call. Her mobile flashed the name 'Sharmila'. She wondered why Sharmila was calling her after such a long time. They had studied together in college and had been good friends. Sharmila knew all about Kalpana's involvement with Agathiyan and its consequences. But, in recent times, Kalpana and she hadn't spoken to each other or met. Before she could answer the phone, the ringing stopped.

Kalpana dialled Sharmila and within two rings Sharmila answered at the other end. "Hi, Kals! Hope all is well. Am I disturbing you at work?"

When she heard Sharmila's voice, Kalpana felt happy. For anyone, reconnecting with old friends brings joy and adds flavour to life, and it was the same for Kalpana and Sharmila.

“Hi, Sharmi, I’m fine and I am genuinely happy to hear from you. I thought you had totally forgotten me!” Kalpana said, pretending anger.

“How can I, Kals? I hope Ahalya is good.” Sharmila was referring to Kalpana’s daughter.

“All good, dear., and I hope you are fine too. You are not practising or working anywhere now, are you?” Kalpana enquired.

“No, no; I lost interest. In any case, this guy is rich enough to manage my needs and wants," said Sharmila, referring to her husband. “How about meeting sometime this Saturday? For lunch, maybe? We can go to Hotel Leela.”

“Great! Let’s do that. Saturday is an easy day for me,” Kalpana replied and confirmed the meeting.

After the call with Sharmila, Kalpana decided to drop Meena at her father’s place that afternoon so that Meena could come back on Sunday night.

Kalpana was buoyed after the unexpected call with Sharmila, though at the back of her mind, she wondered if Sharmila had some agenda for reaching out.

She reached her clinic.

* * * * *

ELANGOVAN

It was eight in the morning. Already, a few key party members were entering the compound of the building that housed the party headquarters. As usual, there were big banners, festoons and party flags lining the route to the office.

There were a few changes though. A notable difference was the prominence given to Agathiyan and Kathiresan, the former getting a little more than the latter. Their faces, and the slogans in their praise on the posters, were significant and visible. Elangovan had given clear directions to his subordinates and they had been executed well. There was some importance given to Pandiyan too.

Key party members inferred that there was something special awaiting the three. With the election date having been announced, the changes in the prominence given to a few chosen faces sent out a clear, unambiguous message to all. The media had already started posting articles online. Speculations were running high amongst political analysts and even the Opposition and Alliance parties.

Elangovan was glued to the television all morning, amused at the visibility his party was getting without spending any money. He deliberately avoided answering all the phone calls he was receiving. He left home at around

11:00 AM. He had directed Agathiyan to go a little earlier in a separate car. A team of ten reasonably powerful people in the party, including Charumathi and another woman, had been instructed to accompany him as Elangovan believed that it would boost Agathiyan's position and image vis-a-vis women.

When Pandiyan and Muthukaruppan entered, there was a flutter of excitement. A few party members welcomed them and walked with them to the meeting hall. Pandiyan was happy, though the support for Kathiresan had undoubtedly irked him. He had no option but to go along with the recommendations and roadmap given by Elangovan. The only solace was that he would be a Deputy Chief Minister and rank above Kathiresan. For the time being, he had to put aside his issues with Kathiresan and present a united front.

When Kathiresan entered, the drums beat out a greeting. Kathiresan had a good number of long-time loyalists and new supporters who sensed that he would become a vital force in the party. Kathiresan had specifically directed his loyalists to create the required stir when he arrived. His command was carried out in earnest and the desired outcome was achieved.

Agathiyan's entry was also celebrated with several members welcoming him at the entrance. Many shawls adorned him one after the other. Slogans of "Long live Chinna Thalaivar (Small Chief, meaning next in command)!" could be heard. Kathiresan, Muthu, Pandiyan and Charumathi welcomed him with folded hands, while Agathiyan opted to hug them. Several shutterbugs went about their jobs, anxious to capture all moments, candid, rehearsed or otherwise. Agathiyan waved to all, avoided speaking to the media, and indulged in conversation only with party members.

Finally, Elangovan entered and the entire place became euphoric. It looked as if the party had already won the election! Elangovan was welcomed with Karagattam, the traditional folk dance, drum beats, several floral bouquets, garlands, shawls and cries of "Our Thalaivar, our Chief Minister." Some even went overboard and screamed: "Long live tomorrow's Prime Minister!"

Elangovan was excited to see all the power centres gathered in one place. He knew his game plan was working well. This was a great start. Despite his ill health he managed to walk briskly. This was what excitement, power and adulation do to people.

After spending some time with the cadres, Elangovan addressed the media, stating that there would be great news soon for all of Tamil Nadu and every Tamilian.

All of them then moved into the large meeting hall. Though it was not a general body meeting, the frenzy and visibility were no less. The agenda was pre-planned.

All cadres had been informed that Elangovan would be the Chief Ministerial candidate and that Pandiyan would be the Deputy CM. A special mention of Kathiresan was made-—that he would play a key role in the upcoming election, and that not only the party, but the people of the State would also benefit from his contribution. Kathiresan felt elated when this announcement was received with thunderous applause.

Elangovan also spoke about Agathiyan, and how he would be the guiding light for several cadres, especially the youth and new recruits. He also praised Agathiyan's administrative and organizational skills.

Everyone, including Pandiyan, Kathiresan, Charumathi and Agathiyan, addressed the gathering. The message was consistently loud, clear and consistent that all of them would work in unity to ensure that the party won by an absolute majority.

There were also a few discussions on possible alliances, seat sharing, etc., as the specially invited cadres voiced their views and opinions. The meeting ended on a high note. Finally, the most powerful members—Elangovan, Pandiyan, Muthukaruppan, Kathiresan and Agathiyan stood together. They raised their joined hands and posed for the cameras, smiling widely. This photograph of the 'Powerful Five' found its way into reputed and not-much-known publications, and was all over social media.

* * * * *

KALPANA

In a very short period, new investments flowed into K Clinic. Kalpana had to dilute her stake to make some money for herself as planned. This was a completely new great-to-have status for Kalpana. Her bank loan was in the process of being closed and her father's property documents would soon be released. She had a decent amount of surplus money for personal use and lots more to come. New clinics were being bought, or acquired on lease, the numbers increasing continuously.

Suddenly the planets seemed to favour her. She thought that perhaps some major changes had taken place in the planetary positions of her horoscope. She had multiple Gods and Goddesses to thank and multiple temples to be visited.

Busy with all this, she forgot to follow up with Sharmila on the meeting proposed by her. She saw a few unread messages and a few missed calls from Sharmila. She responded by apologizing and promising that she would get in touch soon.

Sharmila replied that she would wait. She too realized that Kalpana was becoming busy. There were articles on her and her clinic in the media. She suddenly seemed to be making news.

Kalpana loved every bit of it. She also loved the person who was the reason for all this. Smiling to herself, she called Suraj.

"Suraj, the speed at which everything is happening is driving me wild as well as giving me the jitters! Hope everything will go seamlessly from now. You are there to take care of the business, and, of course, of me. Right?" Kalpana wanted some kind of confirmation from Suraj.

"Oh yes, dear. I 'am always there for you. But darling, we need to be careful henceforth. You will soon start getting noticed and recognized in some circles. It's just a matter of time before you are invited to events, perhaps even as a speaker. You will love the spotlight—but we must make sure it doesn't fall on our personal lives. We must keep it discreet." Suraj's words further boosted Kalpana's confidence.

"So, how do we meet? Er, how do we..." Kalpana giggled.

"Where there is a will there is a way, don't you know? We will manage it somehow." Suraj continued, "How's your day looking?"

"Tied up. I am visiting a few of the shortlisted clinics. I am also figuring out an opportunity to speak and present at a major event. Not here, but in Singapore."

"Wow, K! That's interesting. You never told me about it, but hey, that's the right way to go."

"I will share more details once it's confirmed. You will be the first to know." Kalpana assuaged Suraj's mock anger.

"How is your day looking, Suraj?"

"Very busy... mostly with your work. Remember, we will soon have fifty clinics, and we need money not only to run the clinics but for the huge brand promos. I may even hire a celebrity brand ambassador for K Clinics."

"Sounds interesting... Who could will that be?" Kalpana wondered.

"I may try two or three people, but if we manage to rope in actress Rashmi it will be great. She has a lovely smile, perfect teeth, and a huge fan following. And we need all that. But I'm sure her endorsement doesn't come cheap. Once we reach the shores of Mumbai, we will need to change our brand ambassador. Maybe a Bollywood option... They are even more expensive because of their nationwide acceptance and popularity. And we'll also have to move from regional channels to national media to air our promos. We need big money, dear. Unless we invest big, we can't get big returns." Suraj summed up.

Their goodbyes were exchanged on a note of hope, anticipation and optimism.

* * * * *

KALPANA

Finally, a day was fixed for the meeting between Sharmila and Kalpana at Hotel Leela Palace. Kalpana was in a far better frame of mind since her financial woes had begun to fade; some light was finally visible at the end of the tunnel.

It was a Saturday. After sitting before her open wardrobe for a long time, Kalpana had opted for a maroon Mysore silk saree with a small black border and subtle zari work. The long-sleeved black blouse went well with the saree and she teamed it with oxidized silver jewellery. She back-combed her hair into a bouffant and placed a small black sticker bindi on her broad forehead. Though the attire made her look older, she loved her appearance. This was the last saree she had bought herself, and she had worn it only once before. It made her look very classy. She looked at herself for a while in the long mirror. It felt like the mirror image was jealous of her beauty; she laughed at her imagination.

She took a selfie and sent it to Suraj with the message: "Will call later. Out for lunch with an old friend. And don't worry, it is a 'she'."

"You look like a queen. Have a great day. Shall await your call. And, K, the next time we meet, please wear this. I love the look. You are irresistibly beautiful." Suraj responded instantly. And then got busy with his chores for the day.

When Kalpana reached the lobby of the hotel, she was welcomed by Sharmila, who hugged her warmly and continued to hold her hand for a while.

"You look gorgeous, Kals (that's how Sharmila used to address her in their college days), I am so glad to meet you after such a long time!." Sharmila was genuinely happy.

"Same here, Sharmi, and you haven't changed much except for becoming pleasantly plump. You must be a happy person these days." Kalpana was also happy to catch up with her close friend from the past.

They slowly walked to the Jamavar restaurant in the hotel, still holding hands. They must have looked weird, walking like school girls hand in hand. Perhaps Kalpana had also been missing her friends from way back as she had broken off contact after her affair with Agathiyan.

They placed their order with a liveried steward and started catching up. Sharmila seemed to be in touch with many of the old crowd. She was able to narrate their personal histories and share pictures taken with some friends in recent times. Kalpana was delighted to see them, and saved the numbers of a few, intending to reconnect with them sometime soon.

"Sharmi, I am so glad that you are leading a happy life. You deserve it!" Kalpana smiled warmly.

"Kals, frankly speaking, I didn't approve of my husband's proposal initially but yielded due to family pressure. Two to three years later, I realized it was a good decision. He is not well-qualified, certainly not good-looking, and lacks finesse, but he is otherwise good-natured, well-to-do and is well-connected too. And you know what, Kals? He just can't do without me. I am also happy because that means he can't impress any other woman." Both laughed and started enjoying the food.

Aware of Kalpana's story, Sharmila asked her how she was handling her life all alone. Kalpana shared everything but stopped short of telling her about her newfound relationship with Suraj.

"I am very happy, Kals. Great days are ahead of you. You are a rock star, and I am sure you are going to shine, dear!" Sharmila complimented Kalpana sincerely.

They ordered dessert and waited.

"Kals, as your life is becoming exciting, I am sure you need a companion. Your little daughter, Ahalya, also needs a father. Don't you agree?" Sharmila finally got to the point.

"What do you mean, Sharmi? You want me to get married to someone?" Kalpana was surprised at the turn the conversation was taking.

"Yes, that's what I'm suggesting. But Kals, you don't have to find a new guy; there is ample opportunity to patch up with Agathiyan. I do think it will work out well."

When Sharmila stated this, there was absolute silence from Kalpana.

Dessert arrived, but Kalpana asked the waiter to take it back and directed him to bring hot filter coffee instead.

"What are you saying, Sharmi? I didn't expect this from you at all. Has he sent this message through you? Is he using you as a messenger service? I cannot accept him. You know what he has done to my life, right?" Kalpana was furious but spoke with restraint, keeping in mind that they were in a public space.

"Come on, Kals! I strongly feel it is good for all of you. You will also get back to normal life, and you can build your business big time with his help. It will benefit Ahalya as well to be with her own father. Think about it. I have access to Agathiyan through my connections and I will be happy to unite both of you. Let the world know that Ahalya is a legitimate child and that Dr Kalpana is not alone." Sharmila concluded with this powerful and sentimental line.

To please Sharmila, Kalpana sought time to respond. They left the hotel and agreed to stay in touch as they hugged and said their goodbyes.

As soon as Kalpana got into her car, she called Suraj. "Suraj, I want to meet you tomorrow itself, if not this evening."

"Why the urgency? Any issues dear?"

"Let's talk about it when we meet."

"Okay, dear. Tomorrow we can meet at my place. It is Sunday, anyway."

"Fine."

Kalpana drove home, her mind a whirlwind of emotions and thoughts. How could Sharmila make such an outlandish suggestion? And here she was, thinking that Sharmila had reached out to her for old times' sake. But Sharmila's reaction when she met her, and her happiness at her success seemed genuine. Kalpana finally told herself that Sharmila's affection for her was real, and this marriage proposal was probably some romantic notion that had entered her head and not some devious, pre-planned scheme...

* * * * *

ELANGOVAN

Elangovan seemed highly stressed despite the way he had managed to bring all the key people in his party together. His worries centred around Agathiyan. He wondered if Agathiyan, with his tarnished reputation, could win an election even from a pampered constituency. He had failed in the first rule of politics—keeping one's private life hidden from the media and his political opponents. His opponents, and the media that supported the Opposition, would surely rake up past scandals to discredit Agathiyan before the elections.

Elangovan had the habit of writing down the key points to be addressed. He had less time to attend to these, as the elections were just a few months away. The Opposition, led by the ruling party's Chief Minister, Muruganandam, would use all its resources to buy the media and as many social media influencers as they could. As far as Muruganandam was concerned, there was nothing major to highlight as his Government's achievements were negligible and there were incidences of corruption reported in most of the ministries. In addition, the party did not have a charismatic leader who could swing votes in their favour. For Muruganandam, this was his last chance to continue as CM for another term, and Elangovan was aware that he would go to any extent to win the election.

In Elangovan's opinion, seventy per cent of elections are won with money, unless other emotional and sentimental issues overpower the lure of money. While Elangovan was ready to spend any amount of money, he was afraid that his son's political future would end if the latter didn't wake up to the situation.

Politics is like a jungle and one needs to go beyond the 'survival of the fittest' theme. One should know how to destroy opponents and enemies discreetly and emerge as an acceptable saviour of the jungle. It takes money, muscle power, oratory skills, leveraging the weaknesses of the Opposition, tying up with former foes if that would further the cause, shamelessly speaking for and against certain religious faiths, playing the caste card for political gain, manipulating the media for increased visibility, converting a long-time friend into a foe and vice versa, etc.

Elangovan was feeling even more insecure because of his poor health. He knew that his own trusted colleagues would not hesitate to sideline Agathiyan if the latter did not develop political savvy and became a liability to the party. For the first time, Elangovan regretted that he hadn't groomed his son well enough. Born to an ordinary roadside tailor, Elangovan's hunger for money and power and his ambition and yearning for success were all completely different from Agathiyan's aspirations. This was because Agathiyan was born to a wealthy politician and had everything handed to him on a plate.

While Elangovan had faith in Muthukaruppan and Pandiyan, he also knew that they were consummate politicians and could change colours, especially when they started to prioritize the political futures of their own offspring.

Elangovan thought that Agathiyan would feel the need to deep dive into politics, including public image management, if he had the responsibility of a family weighing on him. The more he thought about it the more he wished that Kathiresan's relative would somehow fix things up with Agathiyan's ex-girlfriend, to ensure that his image was set right in the eyes of the public, especially the women.

He wrote many points, some for discussion with his party men, and some notes to himself.

He couldn't resist a drink and ended up downing two large pegs of Old Monk rum in quick succession. He then smoked a cigarette to ease his stress levels, without caring about how it would impact his already poor health.

He was overcome by dizziness and loss of balance when he stood up. He steadied himself by holding on to the chair for a while.

He dialled Kathiresan; he wanted an update.

* * * * *

KALPANA

It was a hectic day for Kalpana despite being a Sunday. There were a few patients to be attended to. In addition, she had to interview other dentists to fill vacancies in the recently acquired clinics.

She also had to attend a Zoom call initiated by a leading dental clinic chain in Singapore, a contact she developed recently. This was a good professional opportunity and she didn't want to miss out. Later, she was meeting Suraj to share with him the discussion Sharmila had had with her. She had initially wanted to meet Suraj in the morning but then realized that meeting him after completing her tasks would be more relaxing. She wanted to unwind, and she knew that Suraj would be the best company for this.

After reaching her clinic, she finished attending to the patients who had specifically sought Sunday appointments with her. Though she had recruited two more dentists on a part-time basis, some patients still preferred to get her personal attention and were willing to pay more for this. Even while at attending to her patients, her mind kept wandering to her lunch with Sharmila. Kalpana couldn't understand the sudden twist the harmless luncheon had taken. She was struggling to understand what had prompted Sharmila to come up with such an outlandish proposal out of the blue. For herself, Kalpana was not keen on taking it further but she knew that any decision she took should also consider the welfare of her daughter, Ahalya.

She then got into a Zoom call with the chief of a dental chain in Singapore. She had written to them based on an enquiry she found on their website. The company was seeking to associate with dentists in India for mutual sharing of knowledge and services. Kalpana saw some value in this as she knew she could sell her services effectively. She could not only seek patients from Singapore for specific treatments and services but also seek opportunities to train young dentists in Singapore. She carried out a background verification of the company and she found that they were registered with the Singapore Dental Council. There were several positive reviews about the chief dentist and the clinic as well.

She was happy to interact with other dentists from Singapore and India. She also agreed to travel to Singapore to explore opportunities for mutual benefit. She believed that an association with them would help build her company's brand.

She wound up her work at the clinic and asked Meena to go home. She then drove to Suraj's house, reaching in less than twenty minutes. When she entered his home, the usual hugs were missing. Suraj understood that she was preoccupied with something. He brought her a cup of freshly brewed tea. They settled down in the drawing room and began to converse.

"K, do you want anything to munch?"

"No, Suraj. I am fine, thanks." Kalpana replied, sipping the hot tea. She felt better just being with Suraj. Before long, she was pouring out all that was discussed at her meeting with Sharmila.

"Oh sweet! Is this what's disturbing you?" Suraj laughed. That surprised Kalpana.

"Really, Suraj! You find this funny? I am talking to you seriously on a very serious subject. I don't know why all of a sudden this has come up and I am highly irritated about it!"

Suraj sensed Kalpana's anger, confusion and anxiety.

She continued, "It is unlikely that Agathiyan is a better person today. He can't change and he won't change. I thought we were both done with each other. So why this twist in the tale? I'm sure Sharmi wouldn't have brought it up unless it was initiated by Agathiyan. But why? What's behind his sudden change of heart?"

"Relax dear, relax. Let me tell you something seriously." Suraj moved towards Kalpana and sat down beside her. He took her hands in his, trying to calm her down.

"K, I think you must give this proposal some thought. Perhaps this is good for you. It is certainly good for your daughter. Your life will change for the better even if he remains the same kind of person. Remember, you are coming out of your financial crisis and you are building independent wealth now through your business. This reunion will make you not just wealthier, but also powerful. His party is set to win this election, and will be the first family of the State."

Kalpana couldn't believe that Suraj was giving her this kind of dispassionate advice. She was shocked. She had expected a different reaction from him, considering their affair and growing closeness.

"Can't we become a couple, Suraj? I am asking you openly." Kalpana put her cards on the table. Tears sprang to her eyes as the silence lengthened. She jumped to her feet. "Take your time and think about it. Suraj. Let me know your answer in the next three or four days."

She swept out his place, her mind reeling with disappointment, pain and shock.

Suraj didn't respond; he just stood by as she left without bidding goodbye.

* * * * *

SURAJ

Suraj did not wait for three or four days; he wanted to close this chapter soon.

He didn't realize that Kalpana expected him to marry her. He liked her a lot, admired her passion and ambition, loved her company and savoured their physical intimacy, but he was not prepared for a commitment beyond that.

He knew he had to put across this point across to her tactfully. He didn't want to hinder the growth path of K Clinic. The time had come to have an open talk also, about the funding.

It was a Tuesday morning and after his morning gym routine, Suraj called Kalpana. There was no response. At the other end, although Kalpana could see Suraj's name flashing on her new iPhone screen, she didn't pick up the call. There was another call from him within the next five minutes, and this time she picked it up.

"K, are you upset with me for some reason?" Suraj wanted to play safe.

"You are asking me that? It has taken almost two days for you to call after our last meeting on Sunday." Kalpana drew a shaky breath and cut to the chase. "Do you have a response to my proposal???"

"K listen, let's talk about this calmly, dear. I love you very much and you know it. But I'm not ready for marriage. Right now, for both of us, the growth of K Clinic should take priority. You must make your wealth and live well."

"I expected this, Suraj... I expected this. You don't want to get into a commitment, right?"

"Come on, K! Tell me what has been your prime objective till a few months back?"

"Yeah, I wanted to get out of the financial mess I was in and make it big. I wanted to become wealthy, popular and respected. What has that got to do with us getting married? Is my child an issue for you? Be frank."

"Nonsense, K. How can your little child be an issue for me? Do you think I am such a shallow person? But let's put that aside for now and get back to you—apart from wealth, popularity and respect, you now have a fantastic opportunity to gain power too. Look at the big picture!"

Kalpana was confused. "I don't understand, Suraj," she sighed. " I'm trying to see it as you say. Of course, I want to prove myself and that's an unfinished task."

Hearing her conciliatory tone, Suraj was relieved. "Tell you what, K, let's talk further tomorrow evening. We'll drive to my villa on ECR. Anyway, the day after tomorrow is a public holiday so we can stay over and discuss it thoroughly. Suits you?"

"Rascal, I know what you're really after... but, I'll go along with your plans."

The call ended. Kalpana was unable to guess the way forward, but she liked the phrase 'gaining power'. Still, she decided to do her best to convince Suraj, during their stay in the villa, to marry her.

* * * * *

ELANGOVAN

This morning's breakfast at Elangovan's place was a tad unusual. Agathiyan joined his father at Elangovan's request. Elangovan wanted to have a talk with his son, a very serious one, before he left for the party office to meet the district-level leaders.

After the food was served, Elangovan dismissed the domestic staff. He wanted private time with his son.

"Thambi, we need to discuss something very important." Elangovan initiated the discussion. He always used the term 'thambi' (brother) whenever he wanted his son to listen to him with extra attention.

"Yes, Appa. Hope your health is fine?"

"That's precisely the reason for me to talk to you seriously. My health will not permit me to run around much anymore. In politics, if I sit down, I will be put into bedrest by the people around us. It is dirty I know, but that's how I also climbed the ladder.

Now, unless you wake up to reality your future will be bleak. And whatever I have built over the last thirty years will be hijacked by others. Sadly, you are my only son and if you miss out now, you will be gradually removed from the scene, even by my most trusted people." Elangovan set the tone for a long discussion on a very serious note.

Agathiyan understood the situation and he started listening carefully.

"If we have to win this election, I must be the CM candidate and I will make sure you get a ministerial berth though you haven't won any election so far. Neither have you been in real politics and public life, barring attending a few meetings. But, better late than never. It's time for you to be more active now. I have to make sure you get into a leadership position before I collapse or the others who are waiting to grab the seat will push you to a corner before you know it."

Agathiyan was taken aback. He had always held his father in high esteem when it came to political astuteness. He thought of his father as a cunning fox in a jungle of animals.

"Appa, what do you want me to do? You know that I am managing our real estate business and also exploring other business opportunities. I am not exactly whiling away time."

"Our business can be run by people we hire but in politics, it should be our face everywhere. Remember that, else your face will become smaller and smaller not only on posters but also in the minds of the people."

The breakfast was over and Elangovan had eaten very little. He had a feeling of discomfort. He swallowed a few pills and took some time to get out of his chair.

They moved to the drawing room. Agathiyan excused himself for a few minutes to go to the restroom. He also took a few extra minutes to smoke. He dragged a few hurried puffs and rejoined his father.

"Appa, give me a constituency where I can easily win. I can't make speeches and canvas like others do, so I need that advantage. Don't you think people will accept me?" Agathiyan was genuinely concerned, and it showed.

"People will not easily accept you as your face is not familiar to them. Besides, the Opposition will dig up your past affairs, including that dentist, and that will be a huge trump card for them. I understand that she has a child too?" When Elangovan mentioned this, Agathiyan became a bit nervous.

"Alternatively, we'll have to spread stories that she has no morals, and that the child is not yours." Elangovan made it very clear to his son as to what extent they would have to go to.

"Appa, do these things even matter today? How is my private life relevant to the election? Can we not create stories about a bright future... that I am educated, etc., etc.?"

"Don't be a fool. Voters don't want intelligent people or intelligent moves. These people are emotional and they get carried away by these stories. If your story is widely spread, it will not only spoil your chances but also our party's chances." Elangovan continued, "Let me warn you... I trust

Muthu and Pandiyan a lot but they will be different people when something happens to me. You will be at their mercy. They also have hungry grown-up sons at home, and they will leverage every opportunity to gain power." Elangovan did not mince words.

"So what do you want me to do?" Agathiyan was ready for a solution. He was tired of listening to his father lecturing him on his shortcomings.

"Marry that bitch and accept her."

Agathiyan was shell-shocked. "Appa, what are you saying? Why should I?"

"Your reputation is already bad among the public. You have been reckless in not hiding your private life from the eyes of the people. To add to this, there are rumours that you killed your wife, or got her killed. And of course, that you dumped that bitch and she has your daughter. Do you know how this will be ripped in the media by the Opposition? There is only one option... You must marry her, and we will build a great story of sacrifice, women empowerment, etc. Leave that to our team." Elangovan's tone sounded more like a command than advice.

"How will my father-in-law react? Did you think about it?" Agathiyan knew that his late wife's father wouldn't accept this, and would create a scene.

"Don't worry, he will get a seat. He will do anything for that; I know that beggar." Elangovan smirked., "And remember, this wedding with that dentist is a must for the optics. Handle her with care. Understand?"

"Yes, Appa. Noted. And I hope she agrees. She must be wild with me..."

"Again, leave that to me. I will see to all that." Elangovan looked at his watch and hurried to his office.

* * * * *

SURAJ

Kalpana made arrangements at home before leaving for her clinic as the plan was to go to Pondicherry directly from there. Clear instructions were given to Meena. Kalpana lied to her father that she was going to Pondicherry for a college reunion. Her father was happy that his daughter was catching up with her friends.

"Kalpa, tell your friends how successfully you are now steering the business. Try to make some useful contacts. Hope that bastard will not be there at the reunion," he said.

"Thanks, Appa, take care. I will be back tomorrow evening." Kalpana left for her clinic after hugging and kissing her daughter. She purposely ignored her father's reference to Agathiyan.

The day was almost over when Suraj reached the clinic. He had pinged her in advance so that she could come out of her clinic and get into the car. She was surprised to see a new car, or rather, a different car—an Audi Q5, not the usual BMW.

After she got in, she instantly asked him, "A new car? But it doesn't look new."

"No, it is my friend's car, we exchanged ours for a day. I don't want the same car picking you up each time. You will be under observation henceforth." Suraj's explanation created a flutter in Kalpana, but she kept quiet.

Suraj took the East Coast Road. A sudden drizzle enhanced the beauty of the drive once they crossed the city limits.

"So, another hour to your villa?" Kalpana asked Suraj who seemed preoccupied while driving.

"Just another forty minutes. My place is a few kilometres before Pondicherry on ECR." Suraj patted Kalpana on her thigh and smiled.

In about forty-five minutes, at half-past-six, they reached Suraj's small and pretty villa.

Both had a quick shower and while Suraj took a little longer, Kalpana explored the place. She loved the ethnic wooden furniture that adorned the entire villa. She knew that Suraj had great taste, and she was happy that she also fitted into his milieu.

"Come, let's go to my lovely bar," Suraj emerged, looking dashing in a coffee-brown Polo and denim shorts. Kalpana was in her favourite crop top worn over a long black skirt with geometric designs. She looked stylish.

"You look ravishing K, as usual."

"You can hug me and say this, as usual." They hugged each other for a long time like lost lovers meeting after many years. The hugs were followed with an abundance of passionate kissing, till Kalpana broke away.

"Where is your bar? I searched the entire house but couldn't find one. I certainly would love a drink or two before I listen to your points."

"Come, let me take you. It is in the basement. The bar has a bedroom attached too," Suraj wore a mischievous smile.

The bar was small but well-stocked. There were three bar stools, two small tables and six chairs.

"Looks like you come here for private parties, perhaps with your girlfriends..." Kalpana fished for information.

"Trust me, it's been six months since I last came here. I used to come here often with customers and friends, and gradually it tapered down."

She chose to have Grey Goose vodka with cranberry juice while Suraj poured himself a peg of Monkey Shoulder whiskey topped with a splash of water and plenty of ice. After two drinks, Kalpana started the conversation with what she thought was the agenda for this trip.

"Suraj, I thought you would get pissed off when I told you about my conversation with Sharmi. But let me confess, I was disappointed by your reaction. It gives me the feeling that you see me as something to be used and thrown, like tissue paper. Yet... here I am with you, shamelessly." Kalpana poured herself a third drink.

"Come on, K. Please don't talk cheaply. You know I love you very much, and I demonstrate it in every possible way.

I was clear from the beginning that for me marriage is a no-no, however much I love our fabulous relationship. I don't believe in the institution of marriage for many reasons—one of them being that my parents had a bad marriage and my mother went through hell."

"Oh my God! You never shared this with me before."

"Why should I recall bitter past experiences and ruin my present? To cut a long story short, after my father died, I wanted to take care of my mother who was ailing and alone. My elder brother moved to the US, and my younger sister chose her man and migrated to Canada. Both of them never bothered to take care of my mother. In fact, they didn't even come when my mother died. Their condolences were sent through recorded video messages. I didn't marry while my mother was alive because I knew she would feel insecure. I wanted to give her a lot of happiness and peace of mind in her last few years. Post that, I lost interest in marriage and then, after watching my brother and sister struggle with their marriages, I lost trust in this system." He shrugged, "Just my belief, it may still be good for many others." Suraj had tears when he narrated this.

'I am so sorry to hear this, Suraj, I didn't mean to hurt you, you know." Kalpana apologized and the situation improved.

"Didn't your mother want you to get married? Isn't that the wish of all parents?"

"No, not at all. Maybe she was also self-centred. Anyway, that was fine with me."

The topic ended there.

"K, in our first few meetings you made it very clear that you wanted to succeed financially, build wealth, and prove a point, right? This is on account of what you have undergone in life. I can relate to it. This is why I thought that your success was my success, your win is my win. Now I see an opportunity for you to become powerful, apart from just being wealthy," Suraj reiterated his strategy.

"So, you mean to say, I should go begging him to marry me?" Kalpana frowned.

"He is going to do the begging. Your friend was actually sent to beg on his behalf. He needs you more than you need him. In fact, you don't need him at all. His reputation as a politician is stinking. There are other issues as well, including the circumstances in which his wife died. He won't win the election unless he sets things right. And one of the best things he can do is to marry you. A larger part of the electorate will consider this as an empathetic action from his end; that's how they will project it..."

Kalpana interrupted "And you want me to be the scapegoat? I am least bothered whether he or his party wins or loses."

"Listen K, when you join the family, at some point in time, all power will be in your hands. His father is sick, and while he is alive he will want to position his son as a future CM. Someday you could be the CM's wife. Think about it. On the personal side, ensure that he keeps a safe distance from you. Your business will also flourish and grow in leaps and bounds. You can even set up dental colleges in the State. Think of all that, dear."

"Won't you miss me, Suraj? I will miss you for sure." Kalpana was slowly getting convinced, as she yearned for both wealth and power. Besides, she now sensed an opportunity to have the upper hand over Agathiyan.

"Let's focus on the bigger objective; we can always find opportunities for our special moments. One more thing you may not know, the next round of funding will come from our entity in Mauritius, and a major portion of those funds is Agathiyan's father's black money. This is how they multiply their wealth." When Suraj revealed this, Kalpana was shocked. She didn't know how to react for a while. But she understood there were grey shades in business deals. She knew she had to go through this process. Her objective was to win.

"K, you don't have to worry about anything regarding business. I will handle all that for you. Once we get the required funds and set up a network of clinics, we will sell it for a huge valuation, and you can then exit from the business. Meanwhile, you will flourish as the daughter-in-law of the CM, and later, as the wife of the CM." Suraj concluded, and raising his glass, said, "Cheers to that."

"Cheers," Kalpana acknowledged and began visualizing what was in store. She understood from Suraj's advice that she should prioritize her main objective, rather than her relationship with him. He was anyway not interested in marriage.

She gulped down the rest of her drink and snuggled up to Suraj. "I love you, Suraj. I am not going to spare you tonight; I want to gain memorable moments that I can recall for the rest of my life."

She led him to the attached bedroom, undressed him and undressed herself before she was all over him. The night never ended.

* * * * *

ELANGOVAN

After reaching Chennai, Kalpana waited a couple of days before conveying to Sharmila that she was ready to marry Agathiyan. She made it very clear that she was doing so only to benefit her child and nothing more. Sharmila was pleased that Kalpana had agreed. Her conservative mindset led her to believe that marriage was the best option for any woman and was convinced that once they settled down, Kalpana and Agathiyan would be happy together.

The message was conveyed through the right channels and it reached Elangovan.

Elangovan was delighted with the affirmative response from Kalpana. He knew he had already convinced Agathiyan. This positive development would certainly restore public confidence in Agathiyan, and appropriate narratives could be created on different media platforms to convince the electorate, especially women voters, that Agathiyan was a man with a tender heart. People would forget that his wife died under mysterious circumstances. This development would not only help Agathiyan, but also improve the prospects of the party.

He immediately called Kathiresan to thank him. "Well done, Kathir! Your calculations are going in the right direction. I only hope that she doesn't cause us any trouble."

"Aiyya, I'm sure it will all go smoothly. I will also ensure that we create favourable stories in the media to increase Thambi Agathiyan's reputation and image."

"Thanks, Kathir, you will be in my ministry for sure. I will give you a very good portfolio."

Elangovan hung up. He started to think about the allocation of ministerial berths as he was sure that his party would win hands down. He had to reserve good portfolios for Kathiresan, Muthukarrupan, Pandiyan and something for Charumathi. He wondered aloud if he had to create a deputy chief ministership for his son or give him an important portfolio like Finance, Health or Industries. He knew that his legacy would continue and despite his disapproval of Kalpana, he wished that Agathiyan would become a father once again as he wanted one child to be born in his place. To him, Ahalya was a granddaughter merely on record.

The Namathu Puratchi Katchi headquarters was brimming with activity. A few people had been invited for a specific meeting with the top brass. The office walls were getting a fresh coat of paint. A big party flag was proudly waving at the top of the pole.

A visibly happy Elangovan interacted with his party cadre. Many were surprised to see him in a jubilant mood after a long time. They didn't know his mood elevation was on account of the new development which would tilt people's opinion in favour of Agathiyan.

Kathiresan's presence was more prominent than usual, and he had a few supporters around him to exhibit to others that he had arrived. People knew that finally, Kathiresan was on his way up. His group hoped that their caste would gain more representation in the assembly, compared to the seats they secured five years ago. Kathiresan had been denied a ticket last time due to pressure from Pandiyan. Now, the same Pandiyan was seen talking to Kathiresan with warmth. He even hugged him to convey that all was well amongst them. Pandiyan knew that he had to align with Kathiresan. Even among the party cadres, loyalty swings periodically to protect one's self-interest, or rather, selfish interest.

The core group spent time behind closed doors. It was meant to be a strategy meeting and also a measure to boost bonding among members. Discussions centred around the budget required for each constituency, last election's vote share, means to increase the vote share even in the most unfavourable constituencies and alliances, and seats that could be given to others. Many expressed that the allotment of seats to other parties should be kept to the minimum as they had a great chance of winning the election on their own. Just as the discussions were getting intense, Agathiyan made a late entry. Everyone stood up and gave him a thunderous reception. The late entrance had been planned in advance to make sure Agathiyan was recognized as the new power centre.

Muthukarrupan stood up and voiced his views on some strategic moves and he also stressed the need to buy a few media companies, especially those that ran TV channels in addition to YouTube channels. He quoted relevant statistics to show the extent of influence that some of these channels wielded.

"Thalaivarae, we don't have a TV channel of our own so we need to pay one or two channels to promote us massively. And, we certainly need to consider some of the influencers in the digital media space that have huge followings." Muthukaruppan listed some names.

"Muthu, go ahead. Since we don't have our own channel, let's throw some biscuits and bones to the more demanding ones and let these biscuits and bones work for us." Elangovan approved his suggestions and continued, "Remember to project that we care a lot for our language, our culture and our traditions. Get hold of someone who can speak boldly and loudly and get them to criticize our main rivals. Set up teams to create memes with the objective of provoking hatred towards these people."

Many banged on the bench indicating approval of the suggestions made. As planned earlier over a one-to-one telephone conversation, Kathiresan stood up and said, "Aiyya, Thambi Agathiyan should be our deputy Chief Ministerial candidate. He is educated and young, and this will go down well with the new age voters, especially the youth."

There was silence for a short while as Pandiyan and Muthukaruppan were somewhat surprised. But quickly reading the mood in the room, Pandiyan seconded it strongly, and all applauded. An excited Agathiyan stood up and thanked the people with folded hands.

At the end of the session, all seemed to have ended well. Elangovan's agenda had been achieved. Kathiresan knew that he was in for a big game and both Pandiyan and Muthukaruppan trusted that they would be rewarded, not for loyalty alone, but because in reality, Elangovan couldn't afford to disappoint them.

One by one, people left the venue. Before leaving, Elangovan called Muthukaruppan and said, "Muthu, don't worry about your position and Pandiyan's. I will take care of you both and also, Charumathi. Just ensure that you arrange some good interviews and reports on Agathiyan. In the next three to four months, Agathiyan should gain maximum visibility. We have just five months before the election."

"Definitely, Aiyya." Muthukaruppan knew what he had to do.

Agathiyan hung around there longer, not because he wanted to, but because many wanted to congratulate him and gain his attention. Meanwhile, his phone pinged with a message from someone who was not on his contact list. He moved aside to check the message which read: 'Hi, this is Maya'. He instantly recognized that it was from the model-turned-actress whom he had been pursuing for a long time. He understood that somehow Parthiban had managed to convey his interest. Agathiyan was thrilled. He didn't respond at once but planned to call her when he had the much-required privacy.

* * * * *

AGATHIYAN

Maya was in the middle of shooting and when there was a break she proceeded to the caravan. The Assistant Director accompanied her, holding an umbrella to shield her from the sun. Top actors have the privilege of being pampered.

Once inside the caravan, Maya checked her phone for messages and calls, and to track responses and feedback to her latest posts on Instagram. She had over three million followers on Instagram and she had to keep them engaged to ensure that she was relevant and sought after.

She noticed a missed call from Agathiyan. Without a second thought, she returned the call.

Agathiyan was drinking alone in his room at home, celebrating the visibility he had secured a few hours back at the party headquarters.

When his phone rang and Maya's name glittered on the screen, he was excited. He instantly felt a rush of adrenaline. She had been on his 'most desired' list for a long time. He picked up the call.

"Hi Maya, I'm very happy and rather excited to talk to you."

"Yeah, I wanted to talk to you a few days back, but I've been very busy with my shoot," Maya responded without bothering about his excitement.

"Maya, when do we meet? I assure you I shall make it very exquisite and exclusive. Name any location, anywhere in the world." Agathiyan could not hide his enthusiasm.

"Listen up... I am MAYA. I am a self-made, independent and successful professional. I have got feelers from one or two sources already. I don't need any invitation from you. I know who you are, and you must know who I am as well..." Maya's tone turned a bit tough.

"Hey, come on... just for two days. Quote your price and I won't bargain." Agathiyan persisted.

"Let me warn you... Don't mess with me. I know you are getting married again and you are now being drawn into active politics..." Before she could complete speaking, Agathiyan intervened as he was a bit shaken.

"How... how do you know that?" he asked her.

"Do you think I'm not well-connected? I won't reveal my source, but I repeat—stay away from me!"

"Are you threatening me?" Agathiyan screamed though he was indeed taken aback.

"Just a friendly warning. If I talk to the Press and tell them that I'm being stalked by you, your future will be sealed. I need not even prove anything. Just a statement from me and you'll be finished. I hope you have been following the Me Too movement these days. Just stay away!" she hung up.

Agathiyan threw his phone in anger and screamed aloud: "You bitch!" He gulped another drink. He was sweating profusely though the room temperature was set at 22 degrees C.

Maya had indeed managed to put him in place.

* * * * *

KALPANA

"Appa, I want to talk to you," Kalpana said as she served him hot tea and rusk.

"You can always talk to me, dear child. I can see that you are both very busy and very happy. What can be more important for me?"

"I know, Appa. Now, listen patiently and don't react or interrupt while I am speaking. First, I am happy to tell you that all loans have been settled and this house is free from mortgage. Not only that, I have already made a good amount of money and will make more in the days to come. The expanding network of clinics within this city and in other places is yielding great results. I am diluting my stake in the company which is giving me a lot of money. We can now call ourselves rich."

She smiled. Then sipping her tea and fixing her eyes on her father's, she continued, "Appa, I have some news on the personal front as well. I am going to marry Agathiyan. And it may happen very soon..."

"What? You are going to marry that bastard?!" her father retorted, shock and dismay visible on his face.

"Appa, I told you not to interrupt. Yes, he is a bastard; there are no two ways about it. But there is an offer from this bastard's side for a marriage. I know too that this marriage is for his image-building and is a selfish move, but I am fine with it. More importantly, Ahalya will not be called a bastard. That's important to me. And Appa, I am not the wide-eyed innocent I was. I have learnt about life the tough way and am more equipped to handle the situation now. I know I will be a dummy wife and a dummy member of their family but I will leverage this to my advantage. I am no longer the helpless, submissive Kalpana I once was."

"Can I say something now?" her father wanted to know.

"Please, Appa."

"If this is good for you, it is fine with me. Definitely, it is good for Ahalya. I can manage on my own—Meena is there to take care of me. I hope you will visit me once a month or so. You will belong to a big family soon and I am not sure if you will find time for me. I know I can't visit you; I would not be comfortable and I certainly won't be welcome there. So, remember to visit me whenever you can." His eyes welled with tears.

"Appa, I will come every week and I shall talk to you every day. Try to be happy. You will have a car and a driver to go wherever you want. Live joyfully, Appa. You will miss Ahalya but I will make sure to bring her along with me whenever I visit you." Kalpana consoled her father.

They finished their tea. Kalpana held her father's hands to reassure him that everything would be fine and that she would always be there for him.

"But dear, I thought your happiness was on account of turning your business around... and what about this new friend with whom you talk often? I don't know his name but I think he is a good friend to you." He touched upon the subject subtly.

"Nothing like that," Kalpana said lightly, stood up, and left the room without making eye contact with her dad.

She went to the drawing room where she found Meena studying while Ahalya played with her toys. The TV was switched on though no one was watching. A reporter from a regional channel was reading out the news. After the news ended, Kalpana was surprised to see a promo featuring Agathiyan. The promo loudly announced: "Don't miss this Sunday's 11:00 AM show, the first-ever interview with Dr Agathiyan... Hear him speak about his personal life, political agenda and services to the people."

Kalpana understood what was coming. She knew preparations for the big game were on and Agathiyan was making his move. She smiled to herself.

The promo caught Meena's attention too. She was distracted by the loud announcement and graphics. She abandoned her books and abruptly left the room without a word to anyone. Kalpana switched off the TV when she saw that it had disturbed Meena to the extent that she had run away.

Kissing Ahalya affectionately, Kalpana told her, "Very soon, you will get into the best school, darling."

* * * * *

AGATHIYAN

The Hilton Hotel on Airport Road, Mumbai wore a deserted look at 11:30 AM. Except for a few in-house guests who were dawdling over a late breakfast, there weren't too many people around.

Agathiyan was in the lobby reading the Times of India. Kalpana was supposed to join him for lunch. To avoid any local media coverage they chose to meet in Mumbai. This suited Kalpana as she clubbed this with meeting a prospective franchisee for the expansion of her network in Navi Mumbai.

This lunch meeting was set as the wedding was to happen soon, and Agathiyan wanted to have a face-to-face with her. He offered to send her a flight ticket but Kalpana had refused, conveying that she could afford one herself.

By the time Agathiyan had finished a few phone calls, Kalpana entered the lobby. She was dressed semi-formally in a white top and a pair of stretch jeans, with a checked jacket adding a formal touch.

When they met, there was a not-too-warm greeting with memories of their bitter past surfacing. Agathiyan broke the uneasy silence.

"I am glad you agreed to meet. Thank you."

"Of course. Are we not going to be together soon?" Kalpana tried to make him feel comfortable.

"Yeah, and I hope you are happy about it. I know you must be carrying a lot of resentment towards me."

"See, I don't want to dwell on the past. Yes, I have gone through bitter times; I have struggled a lot... but I thought about it and this reconciliation seems to be in all our best interests. I do understand that you need this marriage more than I do. It will help build your image." Kalpana was blunt.

Agathiyan did not respond. He directed her to the restaurant, indicating that they could converse while dining. They chose a table with the best view. The restaurant, The Brasserie, looked beautiful with its vintage interiors. The many bay windows overlooking the swimming pool presented a perfect setting.

They ordered food, and Kalpana chose to keep it light. She was happy with wild mushroom soup, Greek salad and fresh fruit juice. Agathiyan ordered a reasonably elaborate plate. He offered Kalpana wine, but she refused stating that she had another meeting at 4:00 PM.

"Kalpana, you are quite right—I need this marriage; it will help me regain my image. I am following my father's advice."

"You have always listened to him; I am well aware of it." Kalpana tried but failed to keep the sarcasm out of her voice.

"Let's come to the point," Agathiyan said, dropping all pretence. "This is a marriage of convenience. We will not interfere in each other's lives. Yet, when we are in the public eye, we must project convincingly that we are together in every way."

Kalpana was not surprised. "I am fine if that's how you want it. I can still be a good wife to you, you know. Moreover, this is good for our daughter." She shrugged, "I won't interfere in your life, but I am sure you will mend your ways as you rise politically." Kalpana kept all emotion out of her tone.

"What's her name?" Agathiyan asked.

"Ahalya... and I am pleased to finally reveal her name to her father," Kalpana had a bitter smile when she said this.

"See, you and your daughter... sorry, our daughter, can move into our home whenever you're ready."

"Thanks for the offer, Agathiyan."

"And, Kalpana, you can continue to lead the life you want. I won't interfere in your business. I came to know that some of our money has been invested in your clinics. People told me..." Agathiyan wanted to convey that he was well aware of what was happening in her life.

He continued, "Who is that guy? I am told you both are very close. I don't mind at all as long as you are careful and discreet. No scandals will be tolerated," he warned.

"What do you mean? Suraj is my patient and a good friend who has been helping me with my business. Do you have any issues with that?" Kalpana felt a little agitated. She didn't want Agathiyan to know that she had slept with Suraj. She wanted to maintain her image as well.

"Like I say, I don't have a problem with your friendship or whatever. But after our marriage, you need to handle this relationship carefully. Sleep with him if you like, but do it discreetly." Agathiyan's crude statement disturbed Kalpana. She understood that he hadn't changed a bit. He would continue to be a cheap rogue.

"I would rather not respond to your innuendos, Agathiyan. Let's maintain our respective dignities," Kalpana rose to leave.

"Kalpana, don't be angry. Let's agree to be ourselves. I will get back to you with a wedding date soon. It may be even next month. I must say you look hot even now. I still remember our great times together... and the amazing chemistry we shared in bed." Kalpana cringed when she heard this but kept quiet.

"Why can't you stay?" Agathiyan urged. "I am only leaving tomorrow. Let's relive the great times, dear."

"Hmm, not a bad offer... but I must leave tonight. We will anyway have many good times soon." Kalpana smiled, giving him a feeling that everything would be fine between them.

She left the hotel, and all the way to her next meeting, wondered if she had made the right decision in agreeing to this proposal. She reiterated to herself that her objective was to regain what she had lost. She wanted more; she wanted power. She would not be a doormat, treated like thrash. She wanted an identity and recognition and she was determined to get it.

On her way to the next meeting, she texted: "Hi, Suraj! Let's meet sometime soon."

* * * * *

ELANGOVAN

Discussions were on regarding the wedding date. Agathiyan was not consulted as he was anyhow bound to abide by Elangovan's decision. Elangovan wanted the wedding to be conducted at least three months before the elections which meant they had just one month to go.

Elangovan had invited Kathiresan and Charumathi for the discussion. No other member of the family was invited though Agathiyan had several cousins and aunts.

"Charu, we should ensure that we get all the VIPs to attend, even from the other States and the Centre. The country should talk about this as the best-attended wedding. Be choosy about who should be invited even from our party. The less important members can be ignored. Give the best gifts to representatives from the Media. This wedding should signal to the State that we have arrived, and that we are going to be in power for an indefinite period." Elangovan was full of energy despite his various health problems.

"Don't worry, Thalaivarae, I will take care. This is our family wedding," Charumathi smiled at Elangovan. "But what about Rajendran? Hope he will not create any issue." Charumathi was referring to Agathiyan's father-in-law. Rajendran had been really upset when his daughter died under mysterious circumstances. No case was registered as he didn't have adequate evidence to take on the powerful Elangovan. Yet, he had always suspected Agathiyan's involvement in her death. Subsequently, Rajendran had stayed away from them. He was the leader of a small caste-based party and was distantly related to Elangovan.

"Don't worry about Rajendran. His main wish is to be an MLA before he dies. I will give him one seat that he will easily win with our support. For the rest of his life, he will remain our loyal dog." When Elangovan shared this strategy, all three laughed.

"Thalaivarae, let's invite all and sundry from our party. We will have a separate dining area for them. If we don't take this opportunity and feed them the best of biriyani, we will be criticized. I will manage the crowd; leave it to me. Give them enough booze and biriyani and these guys will work day and night for the next four months. They will feel that you have given them some importance. We need this considering that Agathiyan Thambi is being launched as Deputy CM. I will have my guys manage this crowd the way they should." Kathiresan recommended.

"Hmm. Okay, Kathir. Not just for this election, Agathiyan has to be recognised by every party member at the grassroots level. Please go ahead with your planning. I think we should invite Opposition parties as well. Let them get the feeling that we are a changed party today." Elangovan wore a smirk on his face.

The date was set. The wedding was to be held on June 14, three months before the elections in September.

Elangovan called Agathiyan and said, "Thambi, your wedding has been fixed on June 14th. You have just one month left to prepare. Advance wishes to the future Deputy Chief Minister! Inform that dentist also to be prepared." Before Agathiyan could react or respond, Elangovan hung up.

He then lit a cigarette and smoked it with difficulty. He realized his head ached severely while smoking.

* * * * *

AGATHIYAN

Wedding preparations were on. Kalpana didn't intend to invite anyone from her end. She had very few relatives with whom she had maintained a connection. Her father was not interested in attending the ceremony. She thought this was a blessing in disguise as she knew he wouldn't be treated with respect there. She, however, chose to invite Suraj.

On Agathiyan's side, activities spiked with the wedding preparations. The arrangements were delegated to a few party members who became unusually busy. The list of invitees included politicians from various parties within the State and from other States. Apart from politicians, many other VIPs and luminaries were included from the world of business, entertainment and media. The ruling party was fully aware of the advantage and the visibility that Elangovan's party would get from this event. Chief Minister Muruganandam had already given up hope. He was not unduly worried as he had amassed enough wealth during his regime, for generations to come. He knew he had to wait for five or ten more years for his next chance, and hence his party decided not to spend too much on this election. However, they decided that they would continue to criticize every move of the new Government.

Elangovan personally invited many key politicians and even met Muruganandam at his residence to extend an invitation. The media covered his visit and when people were surprised, Elangovan issued a statement that there was no personal dislike or enmity between them; the differences were only in ideology and policies. His stature went up in the eyes of the public as he projected himself quite well as a changed man.

In the meantime, there were many articles and interviews with Agathiyan. There was also an interview in a popular local magazine covering both Agathiyan and Kalpana. It was a cover story, and since the questions were discussed and structured in advance, the output conveyed that they were both personally delighted. Agathiyan also mentioned here and there that he was pledging his life for the cause of the people, his State and his party.

The wedding date arrived. It became the talk of not just the town but of the State. The end objective was certainly achieved, and there was total frenzy amongst all in the party. New alliances and some secret deals were also negotiated and concluded at the wedding. Surprisingly, many ministers from the Central Government also chose to attend the wedding, as they sensed the need to build a good relationship with Elangovan. Several film personalities also attended the event, including Maya. Agathiyan avoided eye contact with her as her warning was still fresh in his mind. Some leading people from the film industry and a few politicians who did not attend the event tweeted their good wishes for the couple.

Suraj attended the wedding. Kalpana introduced him to Agathiyan, and they shook hands formally. Kalpana expected Agathiyan to treat Suraj badly but she was pleasantly surprised to see that Agathiyan greeted him cordially.

The ceremonies finally concluded and the formal nuptial night was arranged. As per the Agathiyan's wishes, it was held at his own farmhouse.

This was the first time Kalpana was seeing his farmhouse and she could clearly estimate Agathiyan's lavish lifestyle. After a few moments of silence, both started to converse normally. A couple of drinks later, Agathiyan pulled her to the bed. They indulged in lovemaking. Kalpana was not aware that the same bed had hosted many others.

"You are still good!" Agathiyan gave Kalpana a certificate of commendation. She just smiled and reserved her comments. She could not help seeing flashing images of Suraj's handsome face when Agathiyan was on top of her.

* * * * *

ELANGOVAN

While Agathiyan and Kalpana were going through their formal, legitimate first night, Elangovan was celebrating the successful conducting of the wedding and the political mileage derived from it. He knew that the wedding would boost Agathiyan's image enough to safeguard his position and growth. Elangovan, while blessing the couple, blessed his son that he would soon provide him with a grandson to carry on their legacy. Elangovan had a granddaughter but he had no affection for her. He hadn't even seen her yet.

Elangovan was drinking heavily that night, and he called Kathiresan again to appreciate his good work. He also smoked a couple of cigarettes. It was 2:00 AM when he went to bed.

When he woke up in the morning, he experienced dizziness, neck pain and blurred vision. He lost his balance and fell before he could even brush his teeth. Hearing him shout, a couple of servants, including the cook, lifted him and placed him on the bed. Elangovan was unresponsive. An ambulance was called and he was rushed to the hospital.

On hearing the news, Agathiyan and Kalpana hurried to the hospital. Kalpana was not really concerned but pretended to be worried as there were many shutterbugs and videographers from the media, gathered at the hospital. Elangovan was taken to the emergency ward, and then later to the room. Several tests were advised by the doctors attending to him. Agathiyan was advised to go home as there was nothing much he could do. Both of them left the hospital, and Elangovan continued to be monitored for the next three days. Not much information was given to the media, and rumours began floating around that Elangovan had breathed his last.

After three days, Kalpana went back to the hospital to check on Elangovan's status with the doctors. She was told that there was no significant improvement, and though Elangovan was out of danger, he was semi-comatose, unable to move. In addition, his other parameters were also discouraging. The hospital wanted him to be moved elsewhere to avoid riots and damage to their premises. The admission of a key political person who might become the next Chief Minister of the State did not make it easy for the hospital administration to offer normal services to other patients.

The doctors conveyed to Kalpana that in all probability he would be discharged in the next few days, but would perhaps remain a mere vegetable. Though Kalpana maintained an expression of concern, she was secretly pleased. She hated this man who had exhibited such disrespect and disdain towards her, and who was mainly responsible for her pain in the past. She left the hospital and went home feeling vindicated.

The cadres of Namathu Puratchi Kazhagam were downcast in spirit. Their leader was unwell and there were all kinds of conflicting information floating on the grapevine. The elections were around the corner, candidates had to be chosen, the manifesto had to be created and publicized, nominations needed to be filed, and plenty of public meetings had to be strategized. They were not aiming just to win, they wanted to win a minimum of eighty per cent of the seats and make a mockery of the Opposition.

The current situation of Elangovan, their Thalaivar, worried them. His fiery speeches would be missed. The Opposition would become emboldened by his absence. Some believed that there could be some infighting for power. Permutations and combinations were getting discussed. A few of them still had faith that Elangovan would be back at the helm with renewed vigour.

Meanwhile, Elangovan was discharged from the hospital during the wee hours of the morning to avoid any crowding. Still, some people, relatives of other in-patients at the hospital, managed to take videos of Elangovan being discharged and taken home in an ambulance. A little later, the news went viral on digital media. Many shared the video. Some expressed joy, some, surprise, some mocked him, and some expressed disappointment that he was still alive.

There were several prayers and offerings for Elangovan's recovery and welfare. Kalpana participated in some of them, knowing that the media was covering her eagerly. She chose to be part of several events, including poor feeding. She also spoke to several regional TV channels and shared her faith that the party chief would recover soon to serve the people of the state. She liked the media attention. She realized she was gaining visibility and that many of the key party members sought her favour. Many started looking at her with reverence. She also became a registered member of the party.

At home, she went to Elangovan's room where he was bedridden with two caretakers to support him. As she applied sacred ash to his forehead, she wanted to say, "Hey, old man! See, I am also becoming a good politician. I posed as though I was praying for your recovery but in my heart, I want you to remain a vegetable. I love to see you in this state, and that's my actual prayer." Because his attendants were in the room, she could not to speak her wishes aloud but her smirk conveyed the message whether he understood it or not.

Agathiyan had just returned from the party office, looking visibly tired and stressed. Kalpana went closer to him and consoled him.

"These things happen; they are not in our hands. You must be bold and face the situation, Agathiyan."

Agathiyan was surprised at her soft approach and care. She continued, "Considering your father's situation, you need to take the lead now, Agathiyan. If you keep silent, others will leverage the situation in their favour. Let us pre-empt them by going to the party office and declaring you as the chief ministerial candidate. Let's see who objects."

Agathiyan was again pleasantly surprised at Kalpana's interest and enthusiasm. He was not aware that Kalpana wanted power indirectly in her hands too. She realized that she might soon become the wife of the Chief Minister of the State.

* * * * *

KALPANA

Kalpana made arrangements for her trip to Singapore. She updated Suraj on the same. She had a busy schedule in Singapore for two days. Apart from participating as a guest speaker at the conference, she had also fixed appointments with a couple of dental chains in Singapore for possible business alliances. She was excited indeed.

Later, she accompanied Agathiyan to the party office. As soon as their vehicle entered the campus, many crowded around them. It was Muthukaruppan who first greeted them and took them to the meeting room. All the key people were there including Pandiyan, Charumathi, Kathiresan and other prominent members from key districts. They enquired about Elangovan's health with great concern.

"Appa is doing fine but I am not sure if he will recover anytime soon." Agathiyan expressed his grief.

Kalpana said in a soft but firm voice, "He is not fine; let's face facts. Thalaivar is not doing well; he is not conscious most of the time. While we are all praying for his recovery, we need to be practical too. For the coming election, he cannot be the CM candidate..."

Before she could complete the statement, there was an uproar. Some of them could not digest the fact that she was telling it like it is without the usual subterfuge.

"Listen, we can present it however we want to the public, but let us be frank among ourselves. I am sure all the senior leaders here understand the reality. While the death of a politician may win sympathy and win votes, ill health is different. People may not vote for such a leader. We need to field a different, new CM candidate... preferably a young and vigorous one. Under the circumstances, it is certainly Agathiyan who is the most eligible. He will also have the sympathy vote considering Thalaivar's health condition." Kalpana ended her speech and pin-drop silence followed for a few minutes, Kathiresan and Muthukaruppan clapped. All others joined them, proving once again that the herd mentality ruled.

Garlands and shawls were offered not only to Agathiyan but also to Kalpana. Charumathi hugged Kalpana knowing that she would soon become a power centre. She noticed that Kalpana had the ability to create an impact, she had the charisma and language skills. She quickly addressed the gathering: "Thambi Agathiyan will be our next CM. Kalpana will speak at our meetings henceforth. She has the power to draw the audience and, especially, garner women's votes. Long live Thambi Agathiyan! Long live Kalpana Akka!" She then hugged Kalpana.

Just like that, a new political force was born.

Many discussions took place regarding seat allocation and the choice of candidates. Kalpana also participated in the discussions. Agathiyan was surprised at Kalpana's involvement and astuteness. He was seeing a new side to Kalpana.

Before they left the venue, Kalpana thanked every senior leader, especially Charumathi. "Whatever it is, you are older than me and a super senior, you should not address me as 'Akka'," she requested with a smile on her face.

"Come on, Kalpana, in politics all this is normal. I won't be surprised if Agathiyan Thambi also starts calling you 'Akka' shortly. That's how we create brands."

Both smiled at each other in complete understanding.

The next day, Kalpana went home to see her father and Ahalya. She missed Ahalya a lot, and she realized that it wouldn't be possible for her to visit them every day. Her schedule was becoming very demanding. She wanted to ask her father if she could keep Ahalya with her and bring her over on weekends to spend time with him. She was sure that her father would agree, as he knew the importance of a child growing up under parental care.

Her father was extremely happy to see her. Ahalya was thrilled. She clutched her mother tight with her little hands and was not willing to release her. Kalpana sensed how much Ahalya was missing her, though it had been just three days since she had seen her last. Kalpana knelt, hugged her daughter, and kissed her affectionately. Loud enough for her father to hear, she said, “My dearest, don’t worry, mummy will take you with her within the next few days. Till then, I will come here every day.” She then looked at her father’s reaction.

Her father smiled and nodded. “I am glad that you have decided to take her along. I, myself, would have suggested it. Don’t worry about me, I am perfectly fine on my own.”

“Thanks, Appa.”

“I hope things are fine at your end. I keep seeing you on TV. You seem to be playing a visible role in party affairs. Please be careful—it is a world filled with sharks.”

“Don’t fret, Appa, I have learnt a lot and that won’t get wasted. It is my turn to gather more than what I have lost in my life, and I need your blessings for the same.”

She bent to take her father’s blessings.

She then went to the bedroom that she shared with Ahalya. Even after she had left home, Ahalya continued to sleep in the same room, and Meena moved there temporarily so that Ahalya would not be alone. Meena just moved the mobile mattress that she laid on the floor. She had rejected Ahalya’s innocent invitation for her to sleep on the cot in her mother’s place. Meena knew her limits.

Kalpana found the bedroom a tad untidy. She started to put a few things in order and was instructing Meena on how to keep things organized. While she was doing this, she saw a copy of a newspaper which carried her wedding photo along with a brief report. She was happy to see it. She realized that the wedding had received huge publicity. Even the local TV channels had covered the event. Since the report ended with an instruction to turn the page for more pictures, she turned it. The daily had published several photos featuring the VIPs and celebrities who had attended the wedding. As she was going through the photos, she noticed something peculiar. In each and every picture, Agathiyan's face had been crossed out in red ink by someone. She was puzzled. She couldn't fathom who would have done something like that, or why. Had her father done it in a fit of rage?

She picked up the paper and confronted her father. "Appa, why would you do something like this? I know you don't like Agathiyan but isn't this too drastic? He had messed up my life in the past, but now I have accepted him and am already on the path to what I've always wanted. Please stop with this hostility; that's my request."

"Kalpa, do you really think I will go down to this extent? The moment you decided to marry him, I knew I had to accept it. I may not have respect or affection for him but that's immaterial. I am not so childish to resort to defacing him in pictures," he retorted.

"Sorry, Appa... Sorry if I offended your feelings."

As Kalpana left the room she spotted Meena trying to look nonchalant. Kalpana had a slight suspicion that it had been Meena's doing. She asked her straightaway. Instead of responding, Meena rushed to her room and closed the door.

Kalpana sensed that something was wrong. Meena was hiding some key information that she was not aware of. Kalpana immediately called Meena's doctor, the mutual friend who had brought Meena to her. She told her to meet her at the clinic the next day. Kalpana left the place a little worried, and rather perplexed.

When she heard what the doctor had to say the next day, her blood ran cold.

* * * * *

PARTHIBAN

Parthiban was busy cleaning the car when he received the call from Kalpana. Though he had her number in his phone, she had spoken to him only a few times in the past regarding arrangements for Meena. And Kalpana had met him only once or twice before. The doctor friend had mentioned that he was one among Elangovan's numerous staff. But after her marriage she hadn't come across him.

Parthiban had been shocked when news of Agathiyan's wedding with Meena's 'Madam' had been confirmed. He wondered if Kalpana knew Agathiyan's true nature and could only hope that Thambi would change his ways after getting such a beautiful and accomplished wife, though knowing Agathiyan he doubted it.

And now, her name was flashing on his phone.

"Madam? Tell me, madam..."

"Parthiban, I want to meet you immediately."

His thoughts flew to his daughter, "Any problem, madam? Is Meena okay?"

"She is fine, and I always want her to be that way. Do one thing, meet me at Vandalur Zoo this afternoon. Take a bus to get there. I will drive myself and reach the place. Be there at 3:00 PM. Call me once you get an entry ticket and enter the zoo."

Parthiban was puzzled. He couldn't make anything out of these orders. With reluctance, he said, "Madam, I will surely come... but why Vandalur Zoo, madam? If you want I can drive you there. Why drive on your own?"

"Parthiban, just follow my instructions. And make sure Agathiyan does not know about this."

She hung up. She had come to know that Parthiban was Agathiyan's driver cum errand man.

Parthiban was anyway on leave that day as he had a medical appointment. At ten minutes to 3:00 PM, Parthiban got a ticket and entered the Arignar Anna Zoological Park in Vandalur, a place that now fell within the city limits, considering the expansion of the city over the last many years.

He called Kalpana, but she didn't answer. He waited for her to call back.

Kalpana entered the zoo. She had dressed differently so that she didn't get recognized. She wore a T-shirt and jeans. A cap covered her hair and her eyes were covered by shades.

She called Parthiban and directed him to where she was standing in front of the tiger enclosure.

It took Parthiban some time to identify her and when he did, he came up, wondering why this elaborate secrecy was necessary.

Looking around to make sure they weren't being watched, Kalpana jumped straight into her narrative. "Two years back, you took Meena to Agathiyan's farm. Do you remember? You were busy working in the garden and, since Meena was free, you asked her to sweep and mop Agathiyan's room so that the chores could be completed faster. What you didn't realize was that Agathiyan happened to be in the room and I'm sorry to say that animal tried to physically abuse your daughter. Yes! That half-naked guy molested her ruthlessly. The little one initially didn't understand what he was doing. She somehow managed to escape his clutches but not before she was chased and traumatized. She could not even scream; so paralysed was she by fear and shock. She finally managed to get away and reach you. You thought she was sweating a lot because of the work done by her, didn't you?

After that, you found her behaving strangely but you never imagined what had gone wrong. This is the incident that has completely changed your daughter. I came to know of it last night only."

A wave of horror passed over Parthiban on hearing this. He broke into loud sobs. He wanted to shout; he wanted to beat himself. But it was a public place, and all he could see was the white tiger pacing up and down in its cage, roaring now and then.

"What do you want to do Parthiban?" Kalpana questioned him pointedly.

"What can I do, madam? All my loyalty has been trashed and raped by him. I am helpless. Instead of dying in a few months, let me commit suicide tonight. I have nothing left to live for. I cannot bear this shame!" Parthiban raged. "Either I must die or he must!"

"Why do you say that you are dying in a few months?" Kalpana frowned in consternation.

Parthiban told her about his terminal diagnosis and shared his doctor's opinion that he wouldn't live beyond six months to a year on account of lung cancer. He had accepted it, he said, Now his only concern was for Meena and her future.

"Parthiban, I'm sorry to hear this. Let's get a second opinion from another doctor known to me." Kalpana was genuinely concerned.

"No, madam. I don't want to go through all that. I am worthless... I should die... I should kill myself. How can I live after hearing this horrific story from you?! But before I die..."

"Yes, Parthiban?"

"Madam, how can I kill him? How can I harm you... you are his wife!"

Kalpana smiled to herself. Things were working out better than she expected. By telling Parthiban she had hoped to discredit Agathiyan, but now she had an opportunity to eliminate him altogether. She knew that Agathiyan was incorrigible and would be a constant thorn in her flesh. Eliminating him through Parthiban was a chance too good to be passed up. Her mind raced with possibilities.

She turned to Parthiban. "Wife? How can I be a wife to a beast who has done this to our Meena? No, Parthiban. He must not live and destroy more girls like your daughter. If you are dying, send him to hell first!"

Kalpana's suggestion stunned Parthiban.

"Madam, are you sure?"

"Yes, I am. I'm giving you permission. If you want to do some good in the world, kill him."

"Madam, thank you... You are my Goddess. I will kill that animal with my own hands. Let the police hang me; I am not bothered. Instead of dying in my small house, let me die in jail." Parthiban grew emotional.

"Now, listen," Kalpana said, thinking quickly. "I am going to Singapore tomorrow and I will be back the next night. Kill him when I'm away in Singapore. Don't mess up; you have just this one chance. And don't worry about Meena, she will always remain a family member to me. She will be educated and married to some good, worthy man—I will take care of all that." Reassuring him, Kalpana left the place.

The white tiger was now silent. It was feeding on the fresh meat thrown into the cage by the zoo attendant.

* * *

Parthiban left the place with determination on his mind. He had a motive, and he had a huge task on hand.

Kalpana left for Singapore. On the way, she had a brief phone conversation with Suraj. She told him that she would like to sell her entire company within the next six months. She wanted to encash her share fully and asked Suraj to work towards this end. She promised him that they would meet up sometime soon.

That same day, Parthiban met Meena and told her to be ready the next day to accompany him somewhere. He promised her that she would find the outing eventful. He asked her to wear a nice dress and present herself well. He told his daughter that he was going to take revenge on the culprit who had caused havoc in her life and that it would be done in her presence.

"Appa has never gifted you anything, my dear, but this gift will be memorable. It'll be remembered by you all your life." He kissed her tenderly and left the place.

Parthiban called Agathiyan a little later. "Aiyya, I have some good news for you. I have managed to get a fifteen-year-old girl She is good-looking and an upcoming artist too." He could feel a lump in his throat, as he created a story around his own daughter.

"Wow, what timing! My wife is also not in the country, and I am very stressed by all this political shit. Bring her to the farmhouse tomorrow evening. No one will be there. Parthiban, if I have a good time, you will be rewarded very well," Agathiyan assured him.

"Thanks, Aiyya. You will not regret it, you will never get anyone henceforth..." Before Parthiban could complete his sentence, Agathiyan interrupted, "What do you mean... henceforth?"

"No, no, Aiyya... you will never get someone like this henceforth, that's what I meant. The experience you will get will be a once-in-a-lifetime kind!" Agathiyan didn't quite get what Parthiban was prattling about, instead, he praised him for his efforts and hung up.

Parthiban laughed as he realized that he was perhaps the only person in the world to get appreciation in advance from the person he was going to kill.

The next evening he bought half a bottle of brandy and a pack of cigarettes. He went home and bathed. He prayed for a while. He went through some of the pictures taken with his daughter, recently, and in the past.

He switched on the TV and half-heartedly started watching the movie BABA on Sun TV, where his most favourite actor, Superstar Rajinikanth was delivering his signature dialogue, knife in hand: "Khatham Khatham, mudinjathu mudinju pochu" with (Khatham Khatham, what is over is over). Normally, Parthiban would have clapped for this scene even if he was watching alone at home, but he was not his usual self. He whispered to himself, "Sorry, Thalaiva, what is over is not over... I have to complete a task; I have to avenge her; I have to ruin him. I have an agenda to kill tomorrow. Forgive me." He knew that this was the last time he would be watching a TV programme. Tomorrow everyone would watch him on TV; he would be the newsmaker; he would be trending on social media; he would be committing the first, and hopefully, the last, murder of his life.

He dialled a number from his mobile, and said softly, "Sleep well tonight my dear. From tomorrow, you will have a very bright future." At the other end, there was absolute silence and then, a few stifled sobs. She knew she would be picked up late the next evening for a task. One that Parthiban had been mentally bracing himself for, over the last few days.

Parthiban opened the drawer of the old dusty table and picked up the piece that was folded in an old white cloth. He unwrapped the gleaming knife and ran his finger along its sharp edge and pointed tip. He stabbed the air forcefully, practising for the following night.

The next evening, Parthiban prepared carefully for the task ahead. He prayed briefly at a temple on the way to Kalpana's home from where he was to pick up Meena. Agathiyan was already in the farmhouse, relaxing. He had no fear of being caught by his father who was lying almost lifeless in bed, or by his wife who was in Singapore. He awaited his prey without an iota of guilt. Despite having fed his lust with many women, almost all of them inveigled there with indirect pressure or promises of favours, his dream of physical intimacy with a young virgin had been eluding him.

Parthiban picked up his daughter and, before they left the house, he hugged her again and again.

"I am sorry, Meena. I never knew the truth. I never knew what you had undergone. I know how traumatic it must have been. Today is the day I am going to reclaim your happiness. Today will be the end of darkness. You will get to live happily, and you will be always taken care of by madam." His eyes welled with tears.

Meena looked nice. She wore a new dress given to her by Kalpana. Her shampooed, flowing long hair enhanced her looks.

They reached the farmhouse.

Parthiban knew that Agathiyan would be in his large bedroom, in all probability, drinking. He had planned the sequence of action. First, he would hit him hard and then stab him deep. He knew that if he failed to do it right the first time, he could get overpowered. And Meena too would be vulnerable. There was no margin for error. He checked his sharpened knife before entering Agathiyan's bedroom. The knife was concealed in a cloth bag that he always carried.

Meena hesitantly followed Parthiban. She had been instructed to remain silent throughout.

Agathiyan was, as expected, drinking when they entered his bedroom. The room didn't have any natural lighting as all windows were completely shut and covered by curtains. The lighting was also not too bright inside as only one light was on. Agathiyan was in his shorts and opted to be shirtless. Parthiban thought this made it easier for him to stab him in the right place.

Meena didn't even lift her face. She was trembling, afraid to even look at Agathiyan. She knew this place. This was the same room where she had encountered the same animal a few years back.

Agathiyan felt excited. For him what mattered was young prey. He couldn't see her clearly due to the dim lighting, and also because he was already tipsy. He looked her over and asked for her name. Meena stayed silent.

Parthiban was under pressure to complete his mission quickly. This was the first and last time he was going to kill someone. He had never harmed anyone so far in his life. He had to act fast.

Agathiyan looked at Parthiban and commented, "Why are you looking tense? You have done a great job,

Parthiban. Your Aiyya is happy." He continued. "Get me the whiskey bottle I left on the dining table. And then you can go."

Parthiban, sensing the opportunity for another weapon, the bottle, quickly left for the dining room, throwing a warning glance at Meena. He picked up the bottle that was half full.

Meanwhile, Agathiyan approached Meena who stood trembling, staring at the floor.

"Why aren't you talking? Is this the first time for you? Don't worry, I will handle you gently." He was about to put his arms around her waist when he felt a hard blow on the back of his head and fell sprawling on the ground. Parthiban was standing with the bottle in his hand. The terrified Meena fled into a corner of the room.

"Don't go away, my child! Watch what's happening..." Parthiban instructed Meena.

Agathiyan regained consciousness from a temporary blackout. He saw Parthiban with the bottle.

"You bastard! Why did you do this to me?" He tried to get to his feet.

Parthiban didn't stop. He kicked Agathiyan hard a few times and again knocked him to the floor.

"Today is your death day, you nasty animal," he snarled. "I am not granting any last wish either. This girl is my blood, my daughter. You tormented her in this same room two years back. She was hardly fourteen then. Since that day, my little one has not been the same. She is still unable to get past the trauma, you bastard!"

Parthiban's statement terrified Agathiyan.

"Parthiban, let's settle this, I am sorry... I will pay you compensation. Leave me now and go away. If you kill me, you will easily be caught." Agathiyan warned Parthiban.

"Who cares! I am going to be alive only for three or four months anyway. Let me do a noble task, then stay for a few months in jail, and die peacefully." Parthiban whisked out the knife. He could see fear in Agathiyan's eyes.

"This is the most important day in my life. Today, I am atoning for all the sins committed by me on your behalf. I did it only because I wanted a better life for my daughter. Little did I know that you had already ruined her life. You should not live! You are not fit to live! Society should be free from monsters like you. Let me eliminate at least one evil force from this world before I die."

"Parthiban, don't do this! Who will take care of your daughter?" Agathiyan played the emotional card as a last resort.

"Ha ha ha!" Parthiban laughed aloud. "Madam will take care of her. She is my Goddess... She is the one who gave me the green signal to kill you."

Agathiyan was shocked. "Kalpana!" he screamed.

"Don't even mention her name." The furious Parthiban stabbed Agathiyan hard and deep three times. Blood gushed out of Agathiyan. Meena just watched the scene, though she was scared to see it. She had tears in her eyes but they seemed like joyful tears. She ran to hug her father signalling her gratitude.

Parthiban hugged her and told her not to worry henceforth. He asked her to erase the incident from her life.

He then tore her dress a bit and made sure that Agathiyan's fingerprints were on some parts of her body. He told her to remain silent if the police questioned her.

He went to the nearest police station with her and surrendered. He confessed to the police that he had killed him to protect his daughter as Agathiyan was attempting to rape her. He was duly arrested.

The news spread like fire. It was all over the media while Elangovan remained in his bed, blissfully unaware.

There was total chaos at the party office within minutes of the news hitting the media.

The media thronged Elangovan's residence as well as the party office.

* * * * *

KALPANA

Around midnight, Kalpana landed, after abandoning her other programmes in Singapore. She was received at the airport by Pandiyan and Charumathi and whisked away without being tracked by the media.

She reached home and exhibited shock when she saw Agathiyan's body laid out in the large drawing room. She shed copious tears and kept wiping them. The Commissioner of Police was there with his team. She took a briefing from him. Parthiban had recorded a video explaining why he had to kill Agathiyan and uploaded the same on Facebook before he surrendered. That video went viral. Kalpana was shown the video.

"Madam, we cannot do anything. We cannot suppress the facts. He has revealed everything. What do you want us to do? If you want you may take the help of our Home Minister or even the CM," the Commissioner suggested.

The next afternoon, Kalpana went to the police station where Parthiban was in custody. She purposely made it a point to draw media attention to her visit.

Parthiban was in a cell.

She told the senior police official that she wanted to talk to him alone. She was given privacy to do so. She went closer to Parthiban. Parthiban smiled at her and thanked her in a whisper. Kalpana didn't say anything incriminating but reiterated that she would keep her promise.

Before leaving the station, she came to know that Meena was in safe custody. She asked for her to be released and sent home after the formalities were completed.

She came out and addressed the media in the presence of many party people.

"It is all very sad. Parthiban is deeply upset about the episode. He told me that he couldn't stop himself when he saw his own young daughter being molested. No parent can tolerate this. Anyway, the law will take its course. As a woman, it is my duty to take care of his daughter's future. After all, Parthiban has served our Chief, and later my husband, for several years. I will handle my personal tragedy and the party will handle the political affairs. We have to put this behind us and see what we should do for this State, especially for the empowerment of women. The protection and safety of women and young girls will be our priority." Some clapped as she left the place for the party office.

There was a huge crowd at the party office. Most of them were seen wearing black badges. The moment she entered the premises, people raised slogans like "Long live Akka!" She greeted them all with folded hands and walked into the large conference hall. A few key members, including Kalpana, occupied the stage. Pandiyan spoke, followed by Kathiresan. Muthukaruppan and Charumathi were also on stage, along with Kalpana.

Kalpana stood up to talk, and the entire crowd raised the slogan again: "Long live Akka! Long live our Leader!"

Kalpana spoke very briefly stating that her personal loss as well as the party's loss could never be compensated. She then said, "Considering the poor health of our Thalaivar, my father-in-law, and the sudden demise of our young chief, my husband Agathiyan, I am forced to take up the leadership of this party. I offer myself as the chief ministerial candidate as the majority of you have requested it." There was thunderous applause. Kathiresan and Muthukaruppan were not too pleased but they joined the others and clapped half-heartedly.

Kalpana continued, "Though I am facing a major personal tragedy and I don't have any interest in power, I have to take this hard decision to ensure that we win this key election and regain our party's legacy. I have to represent our Thalaivar—it's my duty."

There was applause again.

As she went back to her seat, Charumathi said to her. "Congratulations Akka."

"Can't you stop addressing me as 'Akka'? You are much older than me." Kalpana told Charumathi, though she silently enjoyed the way she and the others had started addressing her.

"Henceforth it will be like this only," Charumathi smiled.

The news was released to the media. It was clear to the world that Kalpana had become the new face of the party, and, in all probability, would be the next Chief Minister of the State.

Kalpana reached home and found that now there were always people around her to take instructions. She went into Elangovan's room and asked the helper to leave them alone for a few minutes.

Kalpana then addressed Elangovan though he was not in a position to hear:

"You bastard! You called me a bitch, right? You gave me the option of being your son's mistress. You know what? I have killed your son and now I am not just the queen of this home, but also of the party that you built. Thanks for giving this on a platter to me. Let me tell you, it's now also up to me how and when you will die. Let me check with the doctor as to how many days you will stay like this. If he says it will stretch on for too long, then I may have to send you up in some other way."

Kalpana called up the doctor and asked him, "Doc, I just wanted to check if I should take my father-in-law to the US for further treatment. Do you recommend that?"

"That will be futile as he is in very bad shape. I will come personally and explain," the doctor said, and Kalpana felt relieved.

"How many more days do you think..."

The doctor understood her question. "No more than a month or so."

"Thank you, doctor. I feel so sorry for him."

Kalpana hung up the phone. She had a wicked smile on her face.

"No need to do anything. Let nature prevail." Kalpana walked out of the house with a couple of colleagues from the party. The Press surrounded her. She addressed them briefly.

"This is an unfortunate incident and I am personally devastated. Our party is also shocked but we will remain strong. The law will take its course, and justice will prevail. It is even more sad that our Thalaivar, my father-in-law, is not even aware of the fact that his son is no more. That pains me a lot. I request all of you to now leave us to grieve."

The media thanked her and asked her about the status of Parthiban.

"I will meet with him and ascertain the facts. If what he claims is true, then I sympathize with him despite my bereavement. For me, the life and welfare of every ordinary person in this State is important. In any case, this family will take care of the welfare of his helpless daughter."

Within minutes, Kalpana was all over the media.

The public hailed Kalpana's true and bold statement. The women sang her praises. They especially hailed her statement that she wanted the law to do its duty without fear or favour.

The last rites were performed. As the flames consumed Agathiyan's body and the smoke rose into the sky, the spark of ambition smouldered into a flame within Kalpana.

She turned and instructed Pandiyan to assemble all the cadres at the party headquarters.

The battle was beginning, but she had already won the war.

* * * * *

AUTHOR'S NOTE

Dear Readers,

You are the reason I write and experiment with my writing. I always write based on some trigger. When something impacts me deeply, I attempt to share my perspective through my narratives, and in the case of fiction, my imagination.

Unlike many authors, I keep hopping from non-fiction to fiction. Out of four non-fiction books, three are on the legendary Rajinikanth, and even the title of the other non-fiction book relates to this iconic personality.

I started writing from 2010 and this is my third book of fiction. My earlier books were in a different genre. My first book, Ready...Steady...Exit is a business story interspersed with humour and romance, served up with a twist. My second book, A Drizzle in the Desert is an emotional drama with an element of suspense.

In this book FLAME. Desire...Vengeance, I have attempted a political thriller with a female protagonist. I hope you enjoy reading the book. You may write to me at write2pcbala@gmail.com or connect with me on social media. I welcome your interaction.

Many thanks to Film Director, Suresh Krissna, and Author, Ravi Subramanian, for their encouraging testimonials.

My thanks to my readers for their support and encouragement over the years.

Thanks also to Notion Press; this is my second book through them.

Finally, thanks to my family and friends.

Happy reading.

– P. C. Balasubramanian

www.ingramcontent.com/pod-product-compliance
Lightning Source LLC
LaVergne TN
LVHW091315150826
845673LV00006B/1652

* 9 7 9 8 8 9 0 6 7 8 6 6 9 *

Contents

1

Right Place/Wrong Time

Buzzz Buzzzz Buzzzz Buzzzzz Buzzzz, a phone kept vibrating as a man was about to drink his coffee.

'Ohhh Boy, this is going to be fun' He said as he attended the phone and said 'Hello'.

'Screw you Mikey, you're just a no good bastard', A woman screamed in high pitch; her voice was audible to the next table through the phone.

'Thank you, I have heard worse than this. Since you wanted the reason why I broke up with you, You have the answer, I could use less drama than your jealousy taking over every time I see a picture of a woman. I have to go Lisa, bye!' He cut the phone and shut it down.

'Women Ehhh?' Michelangelo sighed at the table nearby where a couple were staring at him subtly.

Not the first time they would have seen a drama like this played out in public in Naples, but there is always an element of curiosity which creeps the human mind when it is a couple arguing, especially when the voice of the woman is audible to the next table over the phone.

He sipped his coffee and pulled the chair nearby to the table as he sat down; the sun was shining in his face with a yellowish orange ray beaming inside the shop through the glass. It was a pleasant Saturday morning, almost the end of summer and the start of autumn. Michelangelo's phone buzzed again and he saw it was the same woman who had called earlier, he switched off the phone and started to light a cigarette. He shook his head looking at his phone and turned to his right with one sparrow getting his attention. As he sat there following its movements with a smile on his face, it soon disappeared when he heard a loud crash nearby on the road.

Screams of horror echoed as a couple of the waitresses dropped their trays, people on the road were seen running on his right. He blew the cigarette smoke out of his mouth and got up his chair and made his way quickly out the door to see what the commotion was about. The calm autumn morning seemed to turn into a stormy hailstorm within seconds by what he saw. A dead man was seen on top of a car, thrown somewhere from one of the tallest hotels under construction in the city. On closer inspection, it was found to be the owner of the hotel who was constructing the said building, Silvio Ruggeri; one of the most influential businessmen in the city, a man who isn't short of enemies, with connections on the good and the bad side as every powerful man in Italy was known for.